NUMBERLAND

NUMBERLAND

GEORGE WEINBERG

ST. MARTIN'S PRESS
NEW YORK

Design by Claire Counihan

Library of Congress Cataloging-in-Publication Data

Weinberg, George H.
    Numberland: a fable.

    I. Title.
PS3573.E3916N8 1987   813'.52   86-26273
ISBN 0-312-00170-3

Typeset by Fisher Composition, Inc.

First Edition

10 9 8 7 6 5 4 3 2 1

CONTENTS

NUMBERLAND

1

The Orderly Republic

THIS IS THE STORY of the Republic of Numberland, and its citizens—the numbers themselves—who believed they could exist without us.

Numberland was remarkable in many ways. Imagine Egypt or Rome or Babylon at its height. The citizens of these great empires surely pictured their civilization as immortal. They were proud of its order, its splendor, its reach. But those in the Great Republic of Numberland outdid even such nations in pride, since they knew for sure that individually, as well as collectively, they were immortal.

Naturally, no two numbers were the same height. Some were mammoth, others quite tiny. But such differences, which might have caused problems among humans, presented no difficulties to them. In fact, the citizens took advantage of their variations in size and actually utilized them to make their society run smoothly.

Numeropolis, the capital of Numberland, housed only smaller figures. The giants, who lived far away, were too big even to see their Capital, the very power base of the nation.

Fountains of pink granite graced the greenery of its mall. Near its center lay City Hall, an elegant and airy building for the smaller legislators but annoyingly compact for the bigger citizens.

Years earlier it had been decided that Numeropolis was too small for numbers larger than 200,000 to be allowed to set foot in it. Any bigger number who did so was said officially to be setting foot "on" it and not "in" it.

This ruling followed what became known as "the accident." Numeropolis had long ago been squashed in fury by a huge number from far away who became temporarily irrational. To quote the historian 45454 (famous for his theory that history repeats itself), "The numbers, being immortal, survived, but the city suffered terrible devastation." However, the citizens had rebuilt it, and were now proud of its new construction. The avenues themselves were of different widths, radiating from the center, so that from above the city looked like a wheel with numerous spokes. Buses chugged along its thoroughfares.

It was a holiday. The president of the whole Republic, the former General 777* (he kept the star to remind them of his general's status too), read the Numberland oath. Across the nation the citizens watched him on TV.

> Immortal citizens, we have much to be proud of. We run through every subdivision of mountain and stream. We exist wherever there are trees, and where there are no trees, we exist in blades of grass. We branch through every family, genus, scientific argument, and love relationship that human beings undertake. We reward the loneliness of some with our

dependable truths. Human justice would be inconceivable without us. We are the greatest citizens who ever lived.

The smallest figures in the land, the digits, were assembled in SIX's apartment. When their host switched off the set, Four said,

"That inspires me every time."

"I know, but you can't compare humans to us," said Eight.

"No," a few of them agreed. "We're immortal. They're just temporary visitors on earth. They're here, then they're gone."

They were sitting on leather couches, and the room was stuffy. SIX suggested that they go outside for a walk.

Over a cobblestone street they trooped, the ground beneath them worn to shine by the tread of numbers over the centuries.

There they paused and sat down opposite a statue of 474. He had become famous for his logical proof of their immortality. "No number has ever died: therefore we are immortal."

And, indeed, none of them had ever seen a dead number. Afterward, to demonstrate his thesis, 474 had jumped off a bluff and gone on living. He was awarded an everlasting chair at Numeropolis University for his achievement.

"Aren't humans fascinating!" exclaimed SIX. "There's a lot to admire about them."

Someone else commented, "I don't see it. They die and decay, and we go on forever. What's to admire?"

"Just that," said SIX. "That even knowing they have limited time, they *create*. They don't just quit." Then, as if reflecting on his own words, he said aloud, "Limited time. Imagine

3

that! They must have such courage to go on. . . ." He was filled with emotion.

When his friends looked at him with surprise, he decided that he would find out more about humans, in fact find out all he could, even though the citizens of Numberland held them in contempt.

It was a tranquil, star-speckled night as SIX returned home. Indirect lighting made the tree-lined streets look creamy and soft; the city was deserted but for an occasional random figure.

He watched a licensed giant from far away scrub one of the marble buildings with a huge brush, carefully avoiding the windows. The citizens used giants from bigger cities for such purposes, profiting by their discrepancies whenever possible.

The Law of Ascending Responsibility, upheld throughout the Republic, assigned to bigger numbers the responsibility for smaller ones. Usually they visited at night. Before a parade, for instance, giants would come in and put down benches, and remove debris afterward. In the long run, this made work easier for all those in Numeropolis, and reduced the need for ponderous equipment. Other cities took the same advantage, hiring bigger outsiders, and all were well-run and immaculate. Efficiency was to these figures what sculpture was to Greece in the Golden Age, the measure and evidence of its triumph.

But that night SIX lost sight of the incredible efficiency of his own citizens, trying to imagine the magic of human life and what it was like.

2

SIX Starts His Research

E LECTION DAY WAS COMING. Elections were usually quick in Numberland. The tallying of votes was done by cancellation. Voters were encouraged to find someone in favor of the candidate opposing their own, so that both of them could stay home and not bother to vote. That way pairs of citizens could express their preferences by not voting. There was no cheating, though sometimes a citizen too conscientious to stay home on his own would change his vote to accommodate a friend, so that they could both take the day off. In many elections, the cancellations were so well arranged that the first vote cast was conclusive. This was one of the many ways in which the incredible logic of these numeraries paid off. The citizens had enjoyed suffrage without suffering ever since the method had been devised.

Because Numeropolis, the Capital, was the smallest city, only those tiny enough to dwell there could run for President. The incumbent, General 777, was known affectionately as "dynamite" because of his terrible temper. The citizens forgave him that temper because it subsided almost at once, though rumor had it that he occasionally had to go inside a re-frigerator to calm down. They liked him for his vulnerability. Above all, what mattered to them was that Numberland had never been attacked, and this they attributed to the General. He commanded an army of soldiers of all different sizes, and the public recognized this to be an almost impossible task, and respected him for it. Besides, General 777 had as much cha-risma as a figure could have.

His challenger was the suave Professor 1000, in his frock coat, who was head of the Evens Party and renowned for his education. The Professor proposed an "Erudite Society" and promised the nation "advanced degrees for everyone."

The General was for sports, for drill and hard work. His divisions put on spectacular displays. His platform was that "Every citizen counts"; he was against isolation of any figure as a punishment, maintaining that the number system "utterly depends on all of us." In contrast, the Professor represented those who would permanently isolate a criminal. Though there could be no capital punishment, since numbers were im-mortal, he would send a criminal so far away from society that he would never get back. "No figure is indispensable," he would say in his speeches.

The polls showed the candidates to be close, and the Pro-fessor counted on his final television debate to turn the tide.

During the debate, the Professor shuffled through his papers while the General spoke. When it was his turn, he spoke calmly. "My faith is in education. If the common figure learned more, he could *do* more." He smiled benignly.

"Those are elitist words," insisted 777. "The common figure

is fine as he is. Put you up against a practical problem, and you're just an . . . an . . ." Here he faltered.

"Just *an* what?" asked the Professor, smiling. "Make sure it starts with a vowel." He knew the General had trouble finding words. "And don't look at your Chief of Staff," shouted the Professor. "Think it out for yourself as far as your education will carry you."

"Practical problem," shouted the General, who had been counseled to use these two words whenever he was in trouble. They afforded him time until he found his point. "Remember when you were locked out of your car? You tried to use a coat hanger on the door and ripped the upholstery." He laughed.

They differed on why the nation had never been attacked.

"We're invincible," said the General, whose battalions could keep perfect time, even over water.

"We have no enemies out there," the Professor claimed. "Only ignorance."

Admittedly, the General's battalion had never actually fought. So far it had served only to help locate small figures who on occasion got misplaced in remote territories such as Millionland, when they went there to visit. But the Republic was more than satisfied.

It appeared that the General would have no trouble; however, Election Day was still two weeks off, and much was to happen or there would be no story to tell.

Framed in the bus window were prim brownstones and an occasional swank hotel. SIX was on his way to Numeropolis University to find out more about people. The buses on this particular narrow avenue were for the smallest citizens, and no much bigger number could take one. Vehicles on each lane, the buses and cabs and private cars, even the motor scooters, were the same color, to assist the citizens in finding their right bus or cab. Also, a car on a wrong avenue could be spotted by its color. Seldom was a passenger charged with boarding too big a bus to save time at the risk of his getting lost in the shuffle. As SIX looked out of the window, all the vehicles he saw were blue.

SIX himself was dressed in a green sweater and sneakers, and resembled a student that morning, except that his obvious hurry across the campus distinguished him from the regular students, who dawdled. He was on his way to see 44, the Chairfigure of the Populicity Department.

Passing by a classroom, he overheard an instructor addressing his class. "Nor do we bother with the role of male or female, since we don't give birth. Our population is constant, and I might add, all our members are alive."

When 44 came out of his office, SIX asked him what people were like. He answered like a real academic, beginning apologetically. "Well, there's a great deal we don't know, but I'll tell you what I can. People occupy the same geographical terrain that we do," he said. "But we don't see each other."

"Can we talk to each other?" SIX asked.

"Never. It's a basic rule. A mortal can never talk to an immortal." He was wearing a tweed jacket, and he wiped off his glasses pedantically as he spoke, and stuffed them into his breast pocket, also pedantically.

At the mention of mortality, SIX asked, "At what age do they learn that they are going to die?"

44 answered, "Different ages, I think." He described human

8

cities as well as he he could, and wars and sacrifices made through love. Though SIX did not understand this emotion, he felt sad for people, whose glory is their ability to create even while they are decaying.

The teacher said soberly, "There are some of us who don't believe that people exist at all." He plucked a technical journal from a shelf, and riffed through the pages, and found an article entitled "The Nonexistence of People."

SIX was startled. "But *you* think they exist. Don't you?"

"Yes I do," the teacher assured him.

"Did anyone ever see them?" asked SIX.

"Not really," admitted the teacher.

"Do they see us?"

The teacher was hesitant. "Yes," he said finally. "But we hardly ever reveal ourselves to people, as we did to a tiny boy, a gardener's son, little Karl Gauss, who became the greatest mathematician of them all. His was a magical gift to understand us, bestowed on very few in a millennium." He also mentioned Archimedes and Newton, but was careful to say that all these so-called geniuses were dead, whereas all numbers are alive.

"Are there any geniuses now?" asked SIX.

"Only two, but they will not be heard from." One, he said, was a big-bellied black man who had learned to play the piano and to compose for it, as if by magic in his slum in Oklahoma; he had used his mathematical genius, equivalent to that of Gauss, to save himself and his brothers from starvation. He had played on the church piano and never learned mathematics itself higher than long division, but millions had felt his numerical gifts, subsensibly known them, without being able to identify them. He was aging now.

The other was Elizabeth Smith, a nine-year-old girl who was superior in talent to Gauss.

"It was just a fluke in her case," said the teacher. He told the story of how her father, a tailor and a poor man, had papered the walls of her room with the pages of an old calculus book left in his shop. She had gazed at the pages for hours from her bed and later began work with pencil and paper. After the "fluke," she had found the study of numbers enjoyable.

"Anyhow," said the teacher, "she is about to give up her interest in numbers."

"Why?" asked SIX.

"For a girl to spend hours alone sitting on a stoop and thinking about numbers is considered a sign of mental illness," said the teacher. "She loves us," he added, smugly.

"Does she know she is going to die?" SIX blurted out this question.

"Not yet."

On his way home SIX kept on thinking about Elizabeth Smith. He felt an overwhelming urge to speak to her and tell her not to give up studying numbers.

3

---◆---

SIX Meets Elizabeth

---◆---

NUMBERLAND WAS SO WELL run that hardly a law was broken. 55, the lawyer, who had chosen an office overlooking a dozen dangerous street crossings, nevertheless never found a client: immortality was especially fortunate for him. Architects were out of fashion, because if a city worked it was simply reproduced on a bigger scale and used by bigger figures. All the arts were failing. Theater was dead without death as a possibility. Some plays started well but lost pace with the abruptness of a watch hurled into a bathtub. Paintings were lifeless. Poetry failed. The public had no time for culture, there was too much to do. Numeropsychiatrists were seldom needed. True, there was an occasional case of mistaken identity, the seriousness of which was measured by how many units away from the actuality a number thought he was. But such sufferers found recovery at The Home for Broken Figures.

At the Capital, President 777* called his cabinet meeting to order. It was in the now famous Oblong Room, where so many greats and near-greats assembled. The room was decorated with fancy wood-paneled walls and filled with expensive furniture.

The room had a high ceiling, since the meeting table was not horizontal but vertical. For fairness to all of them, a mahogany board was rested on an inclined plane in the center of the room. It rose sharply from the floor. That way the different committee figures could each choose a seat at a spot where his head projected just above the board. To reveal too much of oneself was considered gauche, to reveal too little by hiding below the board was viewed as hostile. Because of his size, the General sat near the bottom of the board.

After the Oath of Allegiance, the statistician-of-the-month appeared and read his report on the state of the nation. "No crimes of any kind, no lateness, no jay-walking—no acts smacking of human irrationality."

Another figure got up and said, "This is the year we choose the poet laureate."

The General leaned forward as some poems were read. "That's a damn good one," he said about the third one. "Make him poet laureate." Then he said, "Meeting closed. You're all doing excellent work."

The statesfigures packed their portfolios, and listened to the recorded music in the elevator together as they descended; then they went off in different directions and at different speeds, content that the Republic had never been better off.

Lying in bed, SIX's last thought that night was that people are more heroic than numbers. In his dreams he imagined the boisterous gallop of horses, and woke up suddenly. He had a feeling as hopeful as curiosity itself. Then the miracle occurred.

In response to what seemed like a touch, he pressed against the wall of his room, which amazingly reacted with a warm embrace instead of reluctance. He squeezed through it.

Now he was out of doors, standing alone in the blue moonlight. A mist of fine snowflakes eddied everywhere. A thin, icy wind was blowing.

Then, suddenly, SIX found that he was flying! Below, he could see the snow on roofs and caked against the sills of the Numeropolis windows. He was higher than any of the citizens. The pine woods and the lake were getting smaller. He was flying as smoothly as a javelin thrown perfectly toward some target.

Before long, he was higher than the great-crested birds, heading somewhere—he did not know where. Onward he went, over tall mountains, leaving clusters of clouds behind. He felt so confident that he made a quick drop just for fun, and saw the dark ocean currents. Himself a dolphin of the sky, he shouted hello. But all he could hear was the sreech of terns far below him.

The next thing he knew he had come to rest on the lower shelf of a pillar on a bridge. It was a Saturday morning. He saw warehouses and crumbling tenements. The sort of neighborhood Elizabeth Smith lives in, he thought.

Below he heard the clatter of trucks and the belching of engines. Occasional cars rumbled across the bridge. Next he flew over shadowy tenements, some boarded up, and he saw a movie theater and then a row of brick houses with fire escapes in front of them. He noticed one with windows close together and a sunken entrance.

Then he was inside a room whose pale yellow walls were almost completely covered with pages from a mathematics book.

For an instant he was startled to see her. He admired her

trembling beauty. Being mortal, she was marvelously delicate, as he had expected she would be. And she was more complicated by far than any number he had ever seen.

In the room was a small wooden table with a few books on it and an unmade bed, and off in the corner a crib obviously in disuse. She was sitting by the window working on some problem with symbols. SIX saw her write his own name several times.

He was stunned by her tenderness as he looked at her brown braided hair and wide, eager eyes, and the silver brace covering her top row of teeth. She was a living, pulsating human being.

The girl was concentrating hard on the problem. He had promised himself he would not disturb her. Her skin was mellow pink; he had never seen quite that color before.

He heard her say to herself in a low voice, "Now I don't know where that mistake is, and I must find it. . . . Five times four plus three . . ."

Then, suddenly, before he could catch himself, he had blurted out to her, "Don't throw that zero away. That's *something*."

"What!" She sounded startled. "Who said that?" She looked all around the room.

"I did, SIX," he said, and there was a terrible moment while he wondered whether she could hear him.

"SIX," she repeated, startled. "I was expecting you someday."

She took a thin, black crayon from a box and drew an admirable round SIX. It was dark and done on a yellow piece of paper and obviously drawn with love.

"Elizabeth, what do you mean you were expecting me?"

This time she smiled broadly and leaned forward, and addressed herself to the drawing of SIX that she had made.

14

"I thought of you. Well, you see, Daddy doesn't want me to talk about arithmetic anymore. He says I know enough to be a lady."

"I know. That is why I am here."

"What?" She drew back in surprise.

"I mean that is one of the reasons." SIX had not told an exact truth, and he knew this. Now he stammered, as he often did when he spoke too fast. "I mean . . . I mean I'm here because I wanted to come here, to see you . . . and so I did."

He was glad of what he had said.

He continued. "Surely you are not thinking of stopping now, of giving me up . . . I mean of giving up numbers entirely." It sounded like the plea of a child not to be abandoned.

She looked perplexed. But he continued pleading with her not to stop.

"I won't," she finally promised. "I'll keep working."

He looked at her again—the shimmering intensity of mortal life. He was glad she did not know yet.

Suddenly her mother called her, and she said yes and was gone, and he was afloat over snowy rooftops and could see the bridge with its stone uprights and metal trusses. He thought he might duck through one of its arches on his way to the sky. But then the launches were tiny in the great curved bay, and the skyscrapers and tall slab towers and the whole face of the city were far below him.

He knew he was back in Numberland even before the wall sprang up in front of him and threatened a headlong collision. But once more it allowed him through, and he was positive he had not been dreaming.

4

Unrest

WHEN SIX MET some of his digit friends at the club, he told them about his seeing Elizabeth. Naturally, they didn't believe him.

"Only a mortal can talk to one," he was reminded.

"Apparently, that's not so," SIX replied.

Then Five, his slightly shorter friend, made the humorous comment, "Maybe we're mortal too."

"At least you've got an artistic imagination," Eight commented snidely. He was referring to the fact that Five wanted to be an artist, but had found no success in Numberland.

"Impossible," someone else reminded them. "Why hasn't any number ever died then?"

"Why don't you forget humans? They're becoming an obsession," someone else said to SIX. "They don't give a damn about us. They just use us for practical purposes."

As SIX's story spread, many assumed that he had lost his senses. "Talking to a mortal. Only a mortal can do *that*." The idea of "mortal numbers" soon became a joke. However, something was fascinating and frightening about the idea of their possible mortality. A rebellious comic played dead on TV, though most thought it was in bad taste.

SIX's visit to Elizabeth was publicized in the *Daily Printout,* which went everywhere in the Republic. Small and big alike read the newspaper, which was originally printed in Numeropolis in its smallest size, where the citizens devoured it. The papers were magnified for faraway cities. Those giants could not even see the original version and could hardly be expected to pay for one.

The newspaper's very distribution was another of Numberland's great accomplishments. Newspapers to travel to a small figure far away would be carried first by a local courier, who would relay them to a giant a hundred times as big. The giant would then stalk over the hills with them. For still greater distances, the process would be repeated, each messenger a miniature alongside the one to whom he handed his batch of copies. Halfway along would come the tapering off; giants would hand their newspapers down to relative midgets and finally to the local courier, who would make the delivery and get the tip.

A group of giants faraway found SIX's report provocative. Could an immortal really converse with a person? No, it was impossible; this was the consensus. SIX had suffered a strange kind of malady.

"Unless, of course, we are really mortal." This seemed the natural conclusion. "How can we be sure that we're not?" For the first time in the nation's long history, a vague uncertainty insinuated itself. Numberland, which had flourished under the General, was showing the first symptoms of a turmoil that was to assume monstrous proportions.

The earliest signs of this turmoil were subtle. Uncertain

about how much time they really had, the citizens began using time differently. Since the beginning, they had hardly ever jostled one another in the streets; when two of them strolled together it was common courtesy for the bigger one to slow down. The department stores had huge second-story windows displaying bigger clothing so that friends of unequal size could do window shopping while keeping pace with one another. Now some citizens began walking at their own speeds, leaving others behind. Sales figures were curt. These were trivial forms of discourtesy, and yet they were an unmistakable early sign of panic.

Next the possibility of death made an even stronger appearance. It seemed utterly too much for certain individuals to take. Previously well behaved, with immortality in the bag, a few of them here and there suddenly acted irrationally. A museum guard, who had been staring at an ancient but ugly vase for many years, abruptly seized it and hurled it into the wall, dashing it to pieces. Luckily, his union was strong, and he was back at work the next day. A baseball player stopped running at third base, saying it was all pointless. The player was a star on the Numeropolis Immortals. Such events were unheard of in Numberland, and with Election Day drawing close, the General knew they did not bode well for him.

In the Oblong Room, the Statistician of the Month made his report. "We're still by far the most orderly civilization there ever was; however, this was not a good month." He went on to recount a variety of strange occurrences.

The General listened patiently.

"The danger is to our faith," said another figure. "Ideally, we've got to convince them of what they've always known—

that no number dies, that there's nothing to worry about, nothing to fear."

"But no number *has* ever died," said the General, showing a hint of his famed impatience.

"Can we prove that?" someone asked.

"Yes, we can present every figure in the whole Republic."

"How?"

"How? How?" mimicked the General. He seemed flabbergasted at the very simplicity of the question and his inability to answer it.

"We'll have a *parade* with every figure marching in order," someone suggested. The speaker was 793, who had a marked Southern accent. The Cabinet was stacked with odd numbers, because, of course, the General was odd. "We'll all march in the parade," said 793. "That will prove we're all alive."

The General was delighted. "Can you arrange that right away?"

"I think so," replied 793.

At that the General stood up. "Get everyone ready. I want to announce it soon. A parade, and we'll *all* march." He spoke to the group as if it had been his idea.

"What do you mean 'everyone'?" someone asked.

"From first to last. All of us. All the numbers, the units, starting with One. He will lead the parade. How obvious do I have to make it?" said the General.

"That's a tall order," said one of the politicians, picturing those at the end of the line. It was his idea of a joke.

"Let's not have humor now," replied the General.

"Who is our biggest?" asked one of them.

"I thought you knew," said another.

"I feel relieved," whispered a third at the board. "There are a lot of common facts I don't know, but luckily, they don't come up too often. But this one—"

He paused as they looked it up in the Book of Records.

But there was nothing listed under *biggest*.

"Find him!" the General snapped. "We can't have a complete parade without him." With that he thumped the oblong board. Luckily, he wasn't near the top, or the smaller legislators leaning over it would have been hurtled into the air. But as it was, the board didn't budge. The General appointed a figure in charge of finding the biggest, and discovering his identity. "We can't have the populace losing faith," the General commented.

Even as they spoke, there were new hints of panic. The public was becoming unhinged. Breaks from form were reported in new places. Feeling demoralized, many citizens lapsed into indifference. Within days, every business and industry suffered. Schools reported more dropouts. And if someone called an executive at a top firm, he was either "not in yet," "out to lunch," or "gone for the day."

The citizens definitely needed stronger proof of immortality than they had. Without it, more were submitting daily to despair and savagery, like human beings. SIX had done them no favor by talking to Elizabeth.

20

5

***

The General Loses Ground

***

SIX SAW ROMANCE in the idea of mortality. Just to see what it must be like, he went off into the woods alone and pretended to himself that he had limited time.

At first he felt an impulse to hurry off in every direction, and then sadness at the departure of 87, a friend who was about to go far away. He could hear the naked hills chirping with life, and below him he heard the springs released from the grip of winter. With this pretence the very countryside seemed transfigured. Everything meant more now, was keener, richer, better—because it would not last.

But among his friends, only Five, the would-be artist, found the game provocative. Off alone and pretending, as he told SIX later, "I felt as if my very talent were coming to life."

Even so, when the afternoon was over, SIX realized that it had been only in part like a human day. Glorious as the interlude had been, SIX had known all along that he was immortal. He realized that his sadness at a parting, his pleasure at the sight of colors were not as deep as if he were truly mortal. To think that there might be no more days like today, that thought was itself a color that deepened all the others.

At night, he ruminated about Elizabeth Smith. Others worried about their own immortality, but when he thought of mortality, he thought of her. He pictured her writing the symbols for numbers on a pad, and saying his own name fondly in a sentence with other numbers. "Her attitude toward us is right," the Professor of Populicity had said. "She's the best of her generation." Still SIX wondered if he had prevailed on her to continue. If she stopped, he might never hear about her again. He yearned to see her, to speak to her once more. But that last trip just seemed to happen—it had been utterly out of his control.

At the University he was told that the Populicity department had been closed: Professor 1000 had given the order. No more information was to spread about "human mortals," as he called them; it was too disquieting. Such censorship seemed quite a contrast to the very notion of education. Even worse, the Professor had relegated 44 to another school, not a university at all, but one for beginners.

The school was partly concealed by apple trees; SIX raced through the net of sunlight permitted by the branches until it came fully into view. It was an elementary school, with a bright blue roof that contrasted sharply with its red fieldstones.

SIX raced across a lawn edged with myrtle and fern, and was delighted to see 44 on the porch.

44 told him that the pot-bellied musician had died. His voice had become gravelly toward the end, and he had stopped singing. But even in his last years, the sight of him coming into a late-night spot made members of the band re-

member why they had become musicians, and for a time they would feel lucky. The news of his death made millions cry in Oklahoma City and Detroit and Philadelphia and Harlem. "People wept when he played," said 44.

"Why are you *here*?" asked SIX.

"Professor 1000 is punishing me," he said. "He is doing the worst thing you can do to a teacher. He took my tenure away."

SIX did not understand.

"I must wander from school to school forever," said 44. "Tomorrow I will be far away."

"That's terrible!" SIX said.

"Not really," said 44. "I don't feel that way. There will always be new experiences for me. I'll be a rookie wherever I go, a rookie as long as I live."

On his way home, SIX realized that the only genius with numbers actually alive was little Elizabeth Smith. "her attitude toward us is right," the rookie had said.

For a time the whole Republic seemed suspended, as the Plague of Doubt got neither better nor worse. None who succumbed showed signs of recovering their composure. The public saw the General's ads in the *Printout* for their biggest to come forward and declare himself. It would help considerably if they could find him. But it was obvious they hadn't. They wondered why not.

Then someone on the General's staff recognized that the very sight of the ads was demoralizing; he pointed out that the biggest, whoever he was, surely didn't live in Numeropolis, with its restriction on size. And so the ads were deleted from the Numeropolis editions. The same reasoning applied to other cities, each of which had necessary size restrictions. One by

23

one, local editions of the *Printout* dropped their pleas to the biggest, as they realized that he must be too big to be able to read their version of the paper. They would seek him by using special agents whose task was to contact still bigger ones until someone found him.

There were a few hoaxes. 1,000,005 telephoned Numeropolis declaring that he was the biggest. He promised to furnish proof, but before he could, a much bigger citizen denounced him as a "wayward midget," and confessed that he himself had seen figures who dwarfed him.

Such chaos seemed to argue for a whole new style of government, and naturally favored Professor 1000. Election Day was nearing, and the Professor used the confusion to argue for his erudite society. His own learning was a foregone conclusion. Even the opposition admitted that he was the foremost specialist in the Republic at naming things.

"Our real enemy is imaginary," he announced, and promised that education would eradicate that enemy. He would stock bookstores and libraries as never before. He proposed a library system nothing short of miraculous: Every book and article in the Republic would be listed. Even footnotes would be indexed, so that a scholarly figure could tally the number of times he was mentioned. Being in four footnotes, the Professor announced, was equal to receiving mention in one article. Most important, he promised a new Cabinet, studded with intellectuals, who would surely locate the biggest.

True, the Professor's own book went nowhere. It would have gotten top score as a jackknife from a high diving board, but as a publication it disappeared without a splash. Though "publish or perish" had no meaning in Numberland, the Professor wanted an immortal book to grace his name down through the ages. Because he thought in universals, he imagined he was great. His position on people was derisive. He insisted on calling them "human mortals," and he always used the word "former" in referring to anyone dead. Thus he referred to the "former Newton," and the "former Gauss," and soon, he promised, it would be the "former Elizabeth Smith."

During the campaign, he became accustomed to seeing members of the *Printout* wherever he went. They kept within easy reach and were always respectful. And when he spoke, even 499, the editor and chief of the *Printout,* would sit silently, and would nod with rubbery politeness to indicate his intent listenership. When the Professor objected to his cigarette, he put it right out.

Professor 1000 regarded them all as his students. A member of the press, doing a story on him, accompanied him through the most expensive clothing store in Numeropolis; it was elegant and carpeted and cool, and the sales figures were impeccably attired and spoke in low tones. The Professor told them, "I want my apparel to be correct but not fashionable." He emerged in his usual dark lounge coat and stiff white collar. On the lapel he wore a red and white button with two words, "Erudite Society."

To the press, the Professor spoke of SIX as "a malcontent who hugs his curiosity." He said he had no official statement to make regarding whether SIX had really talked to a human being. "But one thing is sure," he announced. "Our citizens are immortal and we will soon prove it." He added that if elected, he would do what was necessary to educate SIX.

Meanwhile, the General stuck to his guns and tried to find the biggest, but it began to look like an empty hope. He could feel his chances for reelection dwindle with each passing day.

6

The Prospect of Revolution

THE NATION HAD UNDERTAKEN the most intensive search in its history, but so far—nothing. This alarmed the public, who put great stock in the capacity of the General's battalions to locate any missing citizen. These battalions had discovered tiny lost figures more than once; why were they having so much trouble finding their biggest? Soon their lavish red coats with gold braid became a symbol of failure, of their inability to locate their biggest member.

A poorly drawn cartoon illustrated their concern. The motto of Numberland was "There's always another day"; it was prominently engraved on the Federal Buildings, and appeared on taxi cabs and even on signs in store windows. The cartoon showed a flock of figures looking at the motto with uncertainty, and the caption indicated that one figure was saying to another, "I'm not so sure."

Obviously, they needed their proof, and in a hurry.

Of course, the General kept promising to locate their biggest, any day, and added that as soon as he did, the Numberland Parade, starting with little One, their figurehead,

26

would begin. It would be the most splendid event in their history. Most still believed him, or wanted to. But a growing number were clamoring for stronger proof of their immortality than that jump off the mountain for which 474 was celebrated.

To give them further reassurance, the General asked for a bigger volunteer to jump off a much higher cliff. He was pleased when 119,744, who was a full-time soldier, offered himself. Because he was so much bigger than his predecessor, it was hoped that his surviving such a leap would boost the nation's morale. To his credit, 119,744 went resolutely to the edge of the cliff and jumped, rotating as he fell. Those watching were aghast as he crashed into the boulders below, but he calmly got up and brushed himself off. He was uninjured. Many reporters were there, and they tried to make much of the jump. But though it sold papers the next day, beyond that it meant little. To the majority living far away, it was the leap of a minuscule figure.

SIX was by then keeping a notebook on people—when they were mentioned, and what they did. Sitting before his simple brick fireplace, he went over his findings and contemplated the long trip he had scheduled for himself. Perhaps the rookie, now far away, could tell him something more.

Then SIX got up, and stepped carefully over the gravel bed to water some of his plants. He wondered, why were people so often present when numbers were mentioned? Funny about people. They seemed to follow numbers around like dolphins after a human ship. Even if no one fed them, they could be seen joyously leaping out of the water, a nose perhaps, a friendly sound, then gone again, only to surface somewhere else, unexpectedly, from the blind and toiling sea. It was hard to picture a long voyage over the warped ocean without the consolation of people.

He heard an eager knock on the door. It was 45454, the historian in the toga. He was exuberant, and actually thanked SIX.

"You sure relieved the boredom around here," said 45454. (He wore the toga to suggest that fashions return, a corollary of his theory that history repeats.) Then he clutched SIX in his enthusiasm. "Come with me," he said, and repeated, "Come with me."

SIX threw on a jacket and joined him.

On the street, the historian walked with polite slowness so that SIX could keep up with him. It was getting dark. As they turned a corner, they could see what looked like the shadows of two huge poplars off in the distance, but they were moving. These were the silhouettes of giants, far too big to come into the city. Observing them, SIX realized that they were carrying stacks of benches toward Numeropolis.

"It's a public meeting to discuss *action*," said 45454 excitedly.

One of the giants had already come close enough so that SIX could discern his features. He stepped carefully over some low buildings and into a parking lot, and put down two huge stacks of benches. Then a swarm of smaller laborers from Numeropolis emerged and began moving them and spreading them out under the trees.

It was one of those meetings at which bullhorns predominate. Sporadically visible in the light of the bonfires were banners with the words "WE WANT CONFIDENCE."

Throngs bustled and pushed. Above the din could be heard voices as the citizens jostled for attention.

"The biggest will never answer," lamented someone.

"Maybe he doesn't know we're looking for him," said another.

"Maybe he doesn't know he's the biggest," said a third.

"The General only wants him to appear to give us more confidence. What's in it for *him*?"

"Right!"

"Maybe he's really dead!" said another citizen, whom SIX recognized as 32, a local banker. In response to that comment, a great moan went up through the multitude.

SIX was surprised to see Five, his artist friend, in the throng and called to him.

"Hello," said Five. "Thanks to you, I'm here."

"What do you mean?"

"Your idea!" Five shouted over the much taller figures who stood between him and SIX. They were pushing their way toward each other.

"I don't understand," SIX shouted.

Five answered, "Your idea. Mortality. The game. Pretending we have limited time."

SIX was baffled.

They were now facing each other as Five said, "With your idea, I'm creating as I *never could before*. Something gigantic is stirring me. It's wonderful—a power I never had."

As he said this, the crowd sundered them, as if a great wave had swept them apart.

However, they spotted each other and came together once more, and Five said, "I think, for the *first time* I can create something *beautiful*, something other numbers will *feel!*" SIX partly knew what he meant—he'd had the same sense after speaking to Elizabeth. He was about to say something over the noise, when once again he was drawn away. Now Five was utterly gone, and in the multitude SIX found himself surrounded by wholly different figures, the terrain looking as different as when desert sands, blown about, result in a whole new topography.

Just then SIX heard a voice boom out his name. "There's little SIX."

He turned, and saw a figure pointing to him.

"We can't blame him for bringing the truth," said the figure, whom SIX did not recognize.

"He's a hero," said a few others; and before he knew it, a big number hoisted him high in the air for the rest to see. He heard many voices far below shouting the stunning words, "He's a hero! He's a hero!"

From his position high in the air, SIX could read placards illuminated by the bonfires far below. One of them said, "2,000,009 IS VERY UNHAPPY." It was an ominous message. Apparently the plague of doubt was not discriminating.

So far the revolutionary group had no real purpose. They had only their discontent to unite them—and some misty vision of change. They had no slogan as yet. However, it was as if they already heard the sound of the sentence, *some* sentence, the rhythm of it, without knowing its words.

At the core of the group were activists so political that they blamed their every lapse of memory on the social injustice of their choice—they were victimized for being tall, or odd, or even, depending upon who they were. This core became a dangerous and boring nucleus of the movement. Still, these activists were more useful than the passive participants, who merely attended and did nothing. Least useful were the delicately unconvinced, who went mainly to have others coax them into becoming more active.

By then, the pushing and the noise were intolerable. SIX felt better when they put him down. He hurried off, glad to be out of their sight.

In the following days, the idea that the biggest was lying dead somewhere in the distant wastes seemed refutable only by their finding him. The concept of death, as a real possibility for them, what the citizens called "the figurative possibility," had made its appearance across Numberland. And the despair was growing steadily.

7

◆━━━◆━━━◆

Voyage to a Faraway Land

━━━◆━━━

SIX EXCITEDLY ASCENDED the steps of the Hall of Records, in whose volumes the location of every figure was entered daily. It was a magnificent building; the entire structure, the dome and the facade and even the steps, were of pure marble. In front of it stood jet-black iron lamps, which accented its whiteness. Understandably, the citizens were proud of this building, which stood for the neatness and orderliness of their nation. As SIX scurried up the steps, the dome soon receded from his sight.

At the top, 86, the librarian, greeted him. "Shhhh," he said, as if SIX had already made too much noise.

He handed SIX a library slip and a pencil, and SIX wrote down that he was looking for 44, whom he now thought of as "the rookie."

The librarian disappeared into another room and returned with a book, printed that day and giving the lower numbers in order; next to each number was his address in the Republic that day. At the right of 44's name was his present occupation:

RESEARCHER. Farther to the right of his name was his present work address: SAND BUILDING, TRILLIONVILLE.

After writing this down, SIX handed back the book. Again the librarian said "Shhhh," as if he lived with the recurrent fantasy of visitors making great bursts of noise. Contemplating the trip to see the rookie, SIX realized it would be a long voyage, and an expensive one. But to see him and find out anything more that he knew about people, anything he had learned, would be worth it.

Early the next morning SIX was in a cab, zipping past the Numeropolis baseball stadium at the outskirts of the city. Soon he saw wayside garages, and then a huge figure off in the distance leaving the Departure Gate. The cab ascended over steel curves and finally onto a dirt road, which went over what appeared to be a huge tray. Once on the tray, SIX got out. Other travelers from Numeropolis, mostly in pin-stripe suits and carrying portfolios, were milling about. Soon the glass bubble over them was closed; it ensured that during the flight none of the citizens would fall out if the Tray were accidentally tilted by the giant assigned to carry it.

Soon that giant came, and they cheered. The lift-off was accompanied not by the roar of engines but by a grunt. SIX peered through openings in the oblong stone wall to observe it. He had left Numeropolis before, but never to go so far. In awe, he watched the fields and bays recede below him, and was startled when he identified the chalk-white building with the cantilevered terraces as the swank Numeropolis Hilbert.

It was a routine trip. The carrier put the tray down once when he stopped at a pay toilet, and then lifted it and kept going. A while later he himself boarded a much bigger Tray and relaxed on it with his burden. Soon he and other carriers his size were looking down at a giant who dwarfed them by as much as they did the Numeropolis residents. They read their newspapers and magazines, unaware of when the next transfer was made to a commensurately bigger giant. And then still another giant, and then another. The citizens could travel enormous distances this way, by a series of lifts by giants of different orders of magnitude.

Finally the descent began. When SIX could see the ground again he thought there was only one carrier underneath, but actually there were three. It was impossible to tell the sizes of things. He had imagined the whole city to be just below, but then he realized, when considerable descent hardly brought it closer, that it was bigger than he had imagined, and that there was still more time to go. Then, just when he gave up guessing, everything stopped over a huge lawn, and the carriers began unloading themselves and their Trays, one by one.

SIX started his long trek across a field. Though it was exceptionally well manicured, for him it was high foliage. He observed a giant mark a spot near him with a huge flag, called an *asymptote*. Use of these flags was a local procedure to guard against the loss of small figures. Even if misplaced, they could not get far.

The appearance of a tiny building told SIX he had arrived. He hurried inside.

44 was alone in his office, at a duplicating machine. He didn't seem surprised to see SIX, though the latter had come an enormous distance. In fact, 44 continued sticking papers in the machine, and then turned around nonchalantly. "What brings you here?"

"To talk to you," SIX said enthusiastically. "Anything more about humans you can tell me?"

"No," said 44 at once. "No. Nothing." Then he put another paper in the duplicator and pressed a button, and it whirred out copies. "There really isn't much to know. I read about your talking to Elizabeth." He yawned. "I had that illusion once too. Too much concentration on mortals."

"What do you mean?" SIX could hardly believe that even 44 believed he'd imagined the whole visit.

"Give it up. Raising doubts, I mean. Forget it. We're immortal even if we don't have proof. Look, I was there."

"What do you mean?"

"With all the hope and curiosity—where you are now. Looking at the flood tide, the ebb tide. Wondering if it could happen to us. That's what the study of human mortals does. It's upsetting. Push it out of your mind."

"What are you saying?"

"Look at people, but don't get too involved. Let them fend for themselves."

SIX was speechless. He noticed the title page of the set of articles that 44 was about to staple together. It read ANALYSIS OF A TYPICAL SAND SHIFT.

44 saw him reading it, and decided to change the subject. With a show of real interest, he asked SIX, "Did you know that 709,796,543,001 grains of sand *shifted* during a recent sandstorm in the Sahara?" He felt it wasn't a truly important fact, but at least it was a fact.

That's interesting," said SIX. "A number without people." Idly, he asked, "How do we know?"

"Dr. Jonas Fleischer of the Geology Department at some

human university, measured it with a sandometer," 44 replied.

"You see." SIX sounded even more excited than usual. "Always people. Even here." Then, growing more agitated, he shouted at 44, "Don't you understand? Wherever there are numbers, there are people. It seems—"

But 44 interrupted. "I'm glad *you* find it interesting." And he started toward his filing cabinet, as his way of saying "This meeting is over." SIX knew that it was. The rookie had become a veteran. They had crushed his morale. As SIX rose to leave, he summoned his best goodwill. "See you soon," he said to 44.

But the latter replied, "Never." He told SIX, "Tomorrow I move again. A three-day voyage every week—to bigger and bigger cities. Tomorrow's is a 27 carrier voyage, I'm told." Then, ruefully, he added, "I'm lost. The Professor ordained it."

"You are *not* lost," said SIX, unable to believe it.

As the tiny office receded behind him, SIX wondered if the trip had been worthwhile. He felt utterly confused. It even crossed his mind that he had imagined his trip to Elizabeth.

On the voyage back it rained as if the sluices of heaven had opened. One carrier almost slipped on the rough spot where 119,744 had made his heroic leap in support of immortality. Finally, the carrier set the tray down on the outskirts of Numeropolis, where SIX waited with the others for a bus.

He was glad to see his brick fireplace at last. It had been a long trip. That night he dreamed about little Karl Gauss, the gardener's son, and tried to imagine what he looked like. Perhaps he resembled Elizabeth Smith and the musician.

8

The Professor Takes Office

THE PROFESSOR, WHO had been coached by a public relations group, made a strong showing on the eve of Election Day. He wore a blue shirt and a tie with a timeless print to indicate his conviction of immortality. His mystique derived from the fact that the less educated never knew the content of the courses they had missed; they readily assumed that he knew whatever they had neglected to learn and that it was important.

Speaking from his desk, with bookshelves lining the walls behind him, he assured the nation that education was the golden road to progress. He referred to the "weakening of faith in immortality" as a supreme form of ignorance; it indicated poor education throughout the Republic. Under his administration, he promised, this would end. Libraries would be kept open all the time; there would be nightly lectures by scholars, and the number of doctorate degrees would double every ten years. Fact and truth would predominate: No known fact would be withheld from anyone. Even the police would be selected entirely by means of a paper and pencil test.

After he spoke, the flashbulbs seemed incessant as he mingled among reporters, answering their questions.

"What about our biggest?" someone asked.

"That's right!" said someone else. And then, referring to the General's project, which everyone had been buzzing about, "Will you retain the Committee to Locate our Last?"

The Professor smiled. "Yes. But their work will be supervised by scholars, by the best minds in the Republic. Things have been entirely too *random*." That last word was a very strong criticism in a society that prided itself so highly on order.

When asked about SIX the Professor replied sarcastically, "Well, even digits have been known to dream." He went on to say that even if humans existed, surely no human could talk to an immortal. "Mortals and immortals stay ever with their like."

On only one question was his answer unsatisfying to the bulk of citizens. A reporter asked him, "Will you retain the School Removal Squad?"

"No. I'll abolish that, I'm afraid." He smiled and wiped off his glasses after he said that.

The School Removal Squad was extremely popular in some quarters; it did exactly what its name implied. To say "School is out for the summer" meant literally that the schools were gone. For the summer, a giant from the Squad would go to smaller cities and remove the schools, leaving in their place a carpet of lawn. All through the term, distressed students would have fantasies of that moment arriving. Some would actually stay up late to watch the event. By the first day of

38

summer, schools across the nation would be gone. However, under the Professor this would stop. "The chance for extra credits is too great a benefit, and too important to the Republic," he explained.

Even before the Professor had concluded, the General turned off his TV set. He surmised that he was finished; the malaise across the country had defeated him. He knew that only an irrational populace would reelect someone with a record like his. One tiny curious figure, "little SIX" as he was known, had been his downfall. If the General had a sword he would have handed it over, then and there.

The next day the Professor won by so much that many suspected the public forgot to cancel. Never had so many votes been recorded. It was even rumored that the biggest, wherever he was, had voted for him.

At the headquarters of the Evens Party, he appeared briefly to thank them. "The odds were against us," he said. "But then they always are." They all laughed.

Though there was hope, the Republic still suffered from a sense of strain, and all looked to the Professor for the national security they once had, or at least imagined they possessed. With his motto, "Facts for their own Sake," he replaced his entire cabinet, except for the General, whom he left there for contrast. The General was the only figure there without a doctor's degree in his field. The Professor required even of him that he take continuous extension courses, which upset him no end.

Yet throughout the Republic, there was a sense of expectation—as if the populace was waiting for the other collective shoe to drop.

Then came an event that so shook the nation that the Professor himself sought help. From the Hall of Records came a phone call: "SIX is missing." The Professor knew at once what it meant. No location for SIX in the Republic was indicated. It must be that SIX was off talking to a mortal again.

The Professor excused himself from the meeting with the lower-ups at the Capital. "Check again," he shouted. But he knew it would be useless.

"I did," beseeched the librarian. "I tell you, he is nowhere in the Republic."

Earlier that day, while pacing the floor of his room, SIX had wondered why people were so often present when Numbers appeared. So often. Or was it always? What could it mean, this strange relationship between mortals and immortals? "People rely on us," said the Numberland Oath. Then he thought about Elizabeth. Could it really have been a dream, as the Professor maintained? If so, he might never see her again. Never. That in itself would be proof of her mortality. "There is no 'never' in Numberland," the Professor had said. "There can be no 'never' where there is 'ever.'" And the Professor was right. But as SIX thought about it, that held only for Numberland. Not for there, where she lived. He had the incredible wish that Elizabeth could dwell here, among numbers, where she could live eternally.

He worried that in her own land perhaps she had already quit her studies. Possibly he had not prevailed upon her to continue. If so, if that were true, he would surely never see her again. He could feel the thrust of it, as if a human parent were going away forever, without saying good-bye. "I feel double alone now," he wrote in his notebook. The knowledge that she was mortal deepened his pain. It seemed not to matter at all that his last visit to her had so shaken Numberland. The vision of her shimmering beauty was all that mattered now, and the human condition, which he knew so little about.

Then it happened again. At first SIX thought he imagined the voices singing sweetly and then the thumping of horses' hooves. But soon he was on the roof of his tiny house, which shrunk below him as if he suddenly looked through the wrong end of a telescope.

This time the mountains were clad in red and yellow. SIX could hear the merry engine of a train, and then saw it scattering puffs of smoke right and left.

It was a different land, that was clear. The same sky, dappled with white fleecy clouds, but something was different. Below, the surface was blue. Then that silver bridge in the distance, and there were bagpipes near it. The vision was an incredible gift on this bright, human day.

As he drew closer, the bagpipes turned into huge smoke-stacks; the horns of traffic blared, the sounds of many wheels on the cobblestones made it hard to hear anything else.

Now SIX could see human beings moving everywhere, some pushing carts of fruit and others crowding them, and he saw them sitting on fire escapes or sleeping with windows wide open.

Once in the room with her, he saw she was full of mirth. She had wanted to thank him. "You gave me courage," she said to him. "You will always be my friend."

She said a "mathematician man" had emerged from the subway, his newspaper under his arm, and stolen up behind her; he had seen her doing a hard mathematics problem on a pad. Then he spoke to her father and took her to see some human professors in the University. One was a woman who talked about geometry to her. Professor Sydney would take her to the cafeteria twice a week and tell her stories of Hypatia and Sophia Kovalevskia and other genius mathematicians. Then they would talk about problems and do new ones together.

At the sight of her joy, SIX exulted. Her eyes danced and her whole face seemed to twinkle while she told him what had happened.

Looking at her, SIX felt that something strange had occurred, which he did not understand. He noticed that the crib was gone and that she had a long-legged stride when she left the room.

Going home, he kept concentrating on what had troubled him, and felt his attachment to Elizabeth Smith deeper than ever. He knew that no matter how hard it would be for his own figures, he had to tell them. Mortality was not what they thought. That special color it gave to life deepened all the others—he *had* to make them understand. He was sure of it now. At the thought of it, he cried. Elizabeth, the possibility that tonight's visit to her was truly his last, that even if not, their visits were numbered—all these seemed inseparable. Then he wept for all three ideas and for the hopelessness of pulling them apart.

The next day he banged on the door of his artist friend Five, to tell him about the visit. His slightly shorter friend lived in the same building one floor below.

To his surprise, even before he could get his words out, Five greeted him exultantly. "You've done it for me, my friend. You have made me an artist at last." Five explained that he had been doing sculpture lately; he said something magical and fresh had come into his work, all in reaction to this new idea about mortality.

Whenever he spoke about art SIX had trouble following him. SIX's own gift was to plumb the depths. He had always been utterly uninterested in the surfaces of things, in a sense dull to them. For example, his own apartment showed that quite plainly. A hole in the ceiling above his desk had been there a long time. And the hole in the green sweater he so often wore was growing to match it.

But though he truly didn't understand what he had given to Five, he was genuinely happy that he had given something valuable to so loyal and so close a friend.

9

The Second Stage of
the Plague

L ATE THAT AFTERNOON SIX headed for the offices of the *Daily Printout*. It was sunny and mild as he crossed the avenue between the rows of glass-and-steel towers; however, the skyline was marred by the sight of giants far away, sneaking home from work early, inconspicuous in their own cities but unmistakable to the smaller figures.

As beauty yearns to be seen, so truth, in this case SIX's account of his latest meeting with Elizabeth, yearned to be told. Even had he known that his report was soon to cause countless cloud-capped giants, far bigger than those on the horizon, to roar in torment, his urgency to uncover the truth would still have hurried him on.

In front of the Printout Building was a marble slab of a number holding up a much smaller one, who was holding a still smaller one, who was reading the paper. Below, inscribed on the slab was the motto of the newspaper: FOR BIG AND SMALL ALIKE.

SIX followed the editor-in-chief, 499, past a row of offices and into a resplendent room, and they sat down.

But when SIX told the story of his voyage to Elizabeth, the editor appeared unimpressed.

"So you say you saw her again," he said. "What do *you* make of it?"

"I don't know," replied SIX. "But there's an incredible mystery here."

"What could it mean?" asked the editor. "You believe we're immortal, don't you?"

"I think we are."

"Think?" The editor looked surprised. He glanced over his desk and SIX saw that a tape recorder had been on. He felt tempted to stop talking, but went the other way. He told the editor the story again, including every detail he could recall, remembering to mention the bridge and other human beings congregating in the busy streets. The editor said nothing. As he was about to leave, SIX insisted, "I was there. And I *know* what I saw and felt."

Later that day, the *Printout* reported SIX's account in every detail, under the headline: SIX'S INCREDIBLE VOYAGE. It also ran two lead stories, both intended to calm the citizens. One called SIX "irrational" and said he had imagined the whole thing; the other assured the Republic of a reasonable explanation. The editorial noted that either way the citizens were immortal, but called for further proof. Of course, they were all alive, but a parade, even a census of them all, would prove the point.

It was as if the Republic had told itself, "This globe of earth rests on a flat rock," and all of a sudden the rock had been removed.

"Only be patient till we offer the proof you require," said the Professor calmly in a speech to the nation. Publicly he ad-

45

mitted no proof as yet. But there would be a parade; he had retained the General in his cabinet to make sure of one, and the General was making real progress, he told them.

However, for the first time in the history of the Republic, death, at least the possibility of death, lay like a noose around Numberland—and the noose was soon to tighten. Strange things began to happen, even stranger than after SIX's first visit. With the possibility of death ahead, and no guarantee of immunity, many citizens started stealing: There seemed nothing to lose. As if mortality had given them new freedom, they chose to do the things they always wanted to do. Others watched them narrowly, gathering courage to do the same. Whatever spirituality had once lifted them to strive for their perfectly rational republic was now suspect. They had simply been sycophants to immortality, currying favor by serving their Republic. Now that the promise might be broken, they tried to outsmart each other and the Republic wherever possible.

Some struggled against their rising sense of futility by seeking a safe shore until the real proof would come. Many began to jog; with stop watches they went as far as they could, as if covering ground could make them immortal. Others went to unauthorized mystics. Defaults were everywhere. Thanks to the Law of Ascending Responsibility, the citizens were able to manage; a few could do the work of many. But then, almost too horrible to relate, several big figures failed to carry out their jobs. Disappointed, they boarded up their homes, and went wandering idly, in an effort to escape the infection of doubt that was sweeping the nation.

Already there were cases of collapse. Word reached Numeropolis that Mr. 2,000,000,002, on a stroll in the fields, giving

46

thought to the vagueness of his future, uttered a cry and suddenly toppled like an obelisk. But for his pipe, which perforated one of his zeros, he would have been unharmed. In the hospital he was pronounced a contemplative idiot.

What the historian 45454 had termed "The Plague of Doubt" had reached its second stage. The numbers found it hard to remain orderly with such uncertainty about their future. The picture of stray figures wandering in every direction, hopelessly, some stomping small cities and still others lost in hopelessly big ones, seemed soon to become a reality.

The most orderly civilization in history was on the verge of ruin—unless someone could restore its confidence.

10

Numero-Psychiatry

WITH THE SPREAD of despair came the sudden growth of numero-psychiatry. In addition to the standard treatment came group therapy. In a group, figures could point out each other's obnoxious habits, an enjoyable pastime not ordinarily allowed. It helped patients to take stock of others less rational than themselves: Even the most deluded could gain confidence this way.

Then, to cope with the spreading despair, the doctors introduced "stadium therapy." A single doctor with a loudspeaker could treat a multitude. The cost per figure was only half as much, which brought it well within the means of the mentally deranged. If the therapist forgot his scheduled hour, leaving a full stadium there without him, those in the grandstands were told that he *had* appeared and that it was their own fault that they hadn't seen him. During such a session, they would turn to one another and ask, "Do you see him?" "Is he here now?" Those who saw him were considered the healthiest.

Then came "video-therapy." The patient could be treated in

his own home and yet simultaneously with others. Some objected that the video-therapist couldn't see his patient or evaluate his progress. But the stadium therapist couldn't either; indeed, often even the old-fashioned private therapist didn't remember all his patients at sight, and had to peek at his schedule book before addressing them warmly by their numbers. Besides, those treated by video-therapy could express themselves during sessions by cursing and breaking furniture in their own homes.

Most prominent in this field was Dr. 200,001. A week after SIX's visit to Elizabeth, the doctor sat in his office, in his silk dress, of faded peach. He looked at his enameled clock, given to him by colleagues in appreciation for his having invented the forty-minute hour. He was getting ready to receive the biggest fee ever awarded. Professor 1000, awed by his reputation, was coming on behalf of the Republic to solicit his insight.

The scene was the Doctor's private office near the Home For Broken Figures, just outside Numeropolis. The Professor said to him, "Well, you've examined many of these victims. What do you think?"

"SIX is on the verge of psycho-toppling the Republic," replied the good doctor.

"We know that. But *how*?"

The Doctor thought a moment. "Chords," he said, rising to adjust his dress under him.

"What?"

"Chords deep inside them. Chords of chaos. SIX has been touching those chords. Return of the repressed. The fear that death may be possible." Each word from the Doctor cost a lot of money, which is why he spoke with forethought.

"So?" the Professor asked impatiently.

49

Doctor 200,001's peach glasses glittered, adding to his mystique.

The Professor squirmed on the black leather couch, a hot-selling item in every size only fifteen years previously. "So what's the solution?" he asked, showing a hint of annoyance.

"My specialty is diagnosis," the psychiatrist said thoughtfully. He had learned in medical school that slowness lent weight to his words. "However," he added, "the only way . . ." He paused to use a chapstick surreptitiously while he thought. It was impossible to know whether the thinking was an excuse for the chapstick or vice versa. At length he said, "We must suppress the source of unrest."

"How?" asked the Professor.

The Doctor's mind had wandered. "Why? *Why?*" he muttered sadly. Then he thought, "How *unfair* it is that I am just *one unit* too big to be allowed to live in Numeropolis." (This trick of fate, which had led him to choose psychiatry, tormented him still. He had hoped his own analysis would help, and then had banked on years of working with citizens much worse off. But nothing helped.) "How sad it is," he thought. "How sad."

The Professor, not knowing he was off course, rephrased his question. "You've examined many victims now. Can any of them return to rationality?"

"Difficult," said the Doctor. "Once the idea of death has come, once the bond with eternity has been broken, one is never the same."

The Professor's alarm was evident. "You mean it's hopeless?"

"I didn't say that." The Doctor fell silent.

Then an incredible, an almost unthinkable idea came to the

50

Professor. "Doctor, suppose we take all messengers of death, anyone who brings doubt in any form, and *remove* them?"

The Doctor replied at once. "No. That can't be done. None of us can be removed from the number system. It's a rule."

"Why not? *Whose* rule?" Before the Doctor could say anything, the Professor rose from his chair. "I mean *remove* the troublemaker until he appreciates that we're all immortal."

"But—"

Now the Professor was headed for the door. He had heard enough. "Thank you, Doctor. Your check is in the mail."

The Professor's leaving was a profound insult to the Doctor, who was a master at ending sessions on the dot. As the Professor stepped into his private car, he felt adamant. He would isolate SIX, he would save the Republic. He would *bury* that dirty little digit. He was exhilarated.

The very next day he sprang into action. He counseled the nation to suppress its doubts. He announced his cabinet, which, true to his promise, was padded with lexicographers, ornithologists, linguists, cartographers—in place of mere politicians. He promised that during his "semester in office" he would redefine dozens of old words. He declared the letter *I*, standing for *immortality*, to be sacred, and it was soon observed adorning official maps, on the medallions of taxi cabs, and in epigraphs on public buildings, where the populace, seeing it daily, could replenish their courage. And he became grave when he spoke of penalties for anyone who "gave life to the theory of death."

His educational program enthralled the country. No matter what anyone wanted to study, if it led to an advanced degree or added to the nation's store of inert facts, it was rewarded.

51

This gave everyone the sense of a ladder, something to be done, more courses to take, which helped them forget the void. Though many felt themselves slipping, there seemed no way for a populace steadily learning to go backward. They delighted in discoveries of any kind, however meaningless.

Learning became prominent in their leisure too. Every quiz show grew important. The public attended theater and concerts as never before. They came to feel that not to read each newspaper and half a dozen magazines a week was taking a major risk with one's future. Wherever they went, the aim was to leave with some significant fact; for instance, during a ballet they would concentrate on studying the playbill to be sure they memorized the names of the principal dancers and the lesser ones too. Who could know for sure which fact might prove vital?

The Professor's cabinet recommended that it was safest not to talk about humans or anything that dies. Leave that to the experts. For the most part, the public cooperated. The subject was unpleasant anyhow, and they took pains to avoid subversive talk about it.

For a time, the notion of death seemed looming, as if afraid to descend on so erudite a populace.

But the Professor had neglected to censor the arts, and already, across the nation, the subject of death brought life to them. Plays about death continued, and seemed to have a kick that others lacked. Poetry on the subject was fascinating. Philosophers who talked about the uncertain future of the numerical citizens as a group had a vogue, becoming known as "the dark philosophers." In these forms of expression, the citizens, still for the most part feeling immortal, could savor the experience of not being so. Sadness over "the ultimate moment" made them feel dramatic, much as "playing mortal" had before that game was banned. Also, sad and stately music came into vogue.

The Professor saw the harm in these works. But he had long been an exponent of the arts, while they were worthless, and he wasn't ready to stifle them yet. Anyhow, it was hard to pin anything on the artists, who had been inspired by SIX.

SIX himself had been quiet since the decree. And, indeed, many imagined that things were getting no worse. But the Professor knew that the public remained on the brink, and that he had found no real solution. He also sensed that worse trouble was coming, and he was right.

11

The Terrible Snow Horse

THE EXPERTS IN THE OBLONG ROOM looked utterly different from the figures they replaced. They wore strict suits and carried books. After the meeting was brought to order the Professor called for the Statistician-of-the-Month to deliver his report on the plague.

No one came forth.

"Where the hell is he?" asked the General.

"Profanity won't bring him here. That's for sure," replied the Professor.

But maybe it did. Just then 69, the statistician, arrived with a huge stack of papers and handed them out. Under the Professor, no meeting could be held without both a graph and a table of results. As the others perused their copies, the General paused over his, pretending to understand it.

The statistician began. "Referring to the first page," he said, "you will note that there is more literacy in the Republic than ever before. However, as you see on page two, the plague has already reached one in four. It's afflicting more and more of those who were picking up the slack." He paused, and then he delivered the worst of it. "At the rate our citizens are collapsing, we have exactly *two months.* After that we're finished. There will be utter chaos in Numberland."

"It can't be that bad," said the Professor.

"I don't make the statistics. I just report them," the statistician replied. Then he repeated, "Two months, that's all we've got."

The Professor looked over at 674, the special agent whom the General had hired to head the Committee to Locate our Last. "Any progress?" he asked.

674 nodded weakly. "Well, we've exhausted the quintillions. But there are much bigger I'm afraid."

The Professor got sardonic. "And last month you said you were *close* with the Trillions." He smiled, as if the whole fault was that of the investigator.

"I'm sorry."

Then it happened. The huge mahogany doors burst open, and into the meeting room advanced several figures in great alarm.

One of them shouted. "All traffic's stopped."

"No vehicles going out," said another.

"Or coming in."

"Worst jam-up in history. The cars and buses aren't even budging at the Departure Gates."

"The mob is frozen in the streets. The citizens aren't *moving.*"

The Professor saw their panic; he tried to address one of them, but the others all chimed in.

"What caused the trouble?" he asked.

At first no one responded, then someone did.

"A . . . a statue," stammered the bewildered figure.

"A statue?" exclaimed the Professor and most of his cabinet.

"Just a statue. That's all."

Little by little, those who were there pieced together the story for the Professor and the others in the room.

In the chaos, apparently citizens had abandoned their vehicles. Cars, trucks, buses of all sizes stood, zig-zagging and at crosswise angles everywhere. Most astounding, the first recruit who came from Higher Numberland to remove them changed his mind at the last minute and just stood there too. Another, almost too big for the job, was doing his best to straighten out the vehicles and put them on other avenues.

Then once again the doors flung open, and someone shouted, "Here's an actual *witness!*"

The crowd parted as he approached. He was a lumpish figure in a poorly fitting tawny jacket, and had a money-holder hooked onto his belt. Everything about him was gross.

"I left my cab at the intersection," he told the Professor.

"Why?" the Professor asked him.

He answered frankly. "To look at this statue."

"Of what?" the Professor asked.

"Of a horse."

"What?" asked the Professor. "A human horse? I mean, the kind humans ride?"

In his anxiety, the taxi driver clicked out a few coins, which struck the parque floor with a loud clink. They waited while he retrieved them.

"It wasn't just me," whimpered the driver. "It was *everyone* in the streets." He told how others emptied out of stores and restaurants to go over and look at it. Shopkeepers, bank tellers, bus drivers, even the police, and others big and small, ceased whatever they were doing to gaze at it. They were too afraid to touch it, but stood before it in awe.

"What was it made of?" asked the Professor incredulously.

"Of *snow*."

With that, it seemed the driver broke down for a moment, but then resumed. "Of snow. Of snow," he shouted. "That's what made it so beautiful, beautiful. The delicate form, melting—in front of all of us, so graceful." He was unable to go on.

Moments later, another actual witness, who had been selling jewelry in the street, said essentially the same thing. "I wanted to turn away," he said. "But its beauty wouldn't let me."

"What the hell are you talking about?" asked someone in the cabinet.

Then another witness replied, "It seemed to be wrapped in music."

That was all the Professor needed to hear. "Whoever made that statue, *arrest* him!" he shouted. "And not just him. *Mortality* was in that statue, don't you see? This will go on and on. Arrest the sculptor. And along with him, arrest SIX. SIX must stand trial for undermining everything we represent."

"We'd better do it fast," warned the statistician.

"Messengers" thought the Professor, mindful of the psychiatrist's words. "We've got to isolate those messengers, the source, stifle them—or we're lost."

Even those who could see no relation between the snow horse and mortality could sense that the end was near.

12

The Trial

E SCORTED BY POLICE through the streets, SIX marched toward the courtroom. He could tell he was entering the building standing for law and order by the cool, correct alternation of its arched and square-headed windows. The structure had a harmonious regularity and justness of proportion.

However, the courtroom itself was much bigger than he imagined. The tiers of spectators seemed never ending. At the very top the dome was ornamented with golden spokes, so far away that they looked like the delicate work of a goldsmith. The audience was full of numeraries and supernumeraries, all in their finest attire. SIX caught sight of Professor 1000, whom he recognized from his picture; next to him was the former Earl of Northnumberland, now in the Republic a mere private citizen, but with more privileges than he enjoyed in the monarchy; on the Professor's other side sat tiny Two with his beret. Many in the huge hall leaned over to catch sight of SIX as he entered, and the room was full of chatter and hum.

Behind a long desk sat Judge 2020, the so-called "infallible judge." After summoning SIX to come forward, he read the charges.

"You are accused of undermining the Republic by casting doubt on our immortality. Do you realize the harm you have done?"

"No," said SIX frankly.

The Judge then beckoned the Prosecutor to begin his case.

2345 came forward, and read a carefully prepared statement outlining the harm that SIX had caused. He mentioned the dignitaries in despair, the misery of individuals across the nation, the mountebanks selling remedies for fear of mortality in the streets, the collapse of distant giants, some with their spirits blotched like the ever peeling barks of sycamore trees, and the abandonment of cities.

Judge 2020 spoke when he had finished. "However, we will forgive you if you agree not to praise anything human, and *never* to talk with a person again."

The Prosecutor put it simply. "I will drop the charges if you stop studying people and recant. They have nothing we haven't got."

"I can't."

"No?" asked the Judge.

"I'd always wonder."

Angrily, the Judge replied, "Then the trial must continue."

The Prosecutor, 2345, turning toward the judge, warned that he would be requesting the maximum penalty in Numberland: permanent imprisonment. "We can have no death penalty here," he said. "You are fortunate."

He called forth the first witness, an author whose books were required in the schools. "Exactly. There is no prestige in being human. Humans revolve around us. They tally people

59

and poplars by number. We stand alone. Our *independence* makes us superior." This was the party line; having stated it, he stepped down.

After a series of others like him came the star witness, the Expert on Human Pretense. He was a popular TV figure, and SIX hated to see him on the other side. SIX was surprised to observe that he had a mop of tumbled black hair.

"But numbers don't have hair," said the Prosecutor.

"Quite right. It's a wig." And he doffed it with a flourish. "That's what human pretense is." He laughed and went on.

"Time left is their most taboo topic. Their young often shun their old, just because they're reminded of time left. The old have much less time, and the young don't like to think about it. But, of course, we can talk about time easily. We do not go the way of nature—you know what I mean, die."

The citizens were rapt as he spoke. Not the slightest sound could be heard, as the witness elaborated.

"To them, anything that looks wrinkled means 'less time left,' and that upsets them. Most pretend to themselves that they're immortal. They find their state intolerable. Or, secretly knowing the truth, they pretend their children are themselves, that what their children will do after they've died is their own act. They push their children around plenty in the early years so this will work. A few actually get frozen. Some day when their fatal disease is cured, they hope, their blood will be put back and they'll get a few more years; meanwhile they can pretend it will go on forever. Others hurry to get out the music that's inside of them, as if doing that could make up for death."

"And what about geniuses?" The Prosecutor asked this obviously leading question.

"They're weeds, dying out. A few here and there."

It was a dazzling presentation, and he stepped down.

Would SIX now take the stand?

The Prosecutor addressed him. "Immortal SIX," he began. "This is a very serious charge against you. One that carries mandatory imprisonment. Undermining our faith in immortality. Now we all know that humans die. Therefore their lives are worthless.

"No," replied SIX. "That's just the point. Death makes things special."

Now the courtroom became full of noise. The many writers dove into their notebooks. The artist for the *Printout* had been studying SIX through field glasses; after scrawling a few contour lines he rubbed his gum eraser furiously over his sketch pad.

"There's something magical in mortality," SIX went on. "I've got to discover what it is. Please give me just a little more time."

2020 broke in. If a frown could have caused the great chandelier to tumble down over the audience, his would have. He looked furious. "No!" he boomed. "Treason means prison. By your visits, by your whole attitude, you have weakened the faith. But only temporarily—"

SIX had the audacity to speak again. "With just a little more information, I can restore that faith. I promise." What did he mean? SIX hardly knew what he had said or why he believed it was so. But the words were out, and he went on.

"If you let me go on with my studies, I am sure I can help you."

"Help us with what?" said the Judge disdainfully.

"Figure out the mystery."

"Can you help us restore the public confidence?"

"Yes."

"And get the parade started?"

SIX paused for a moment. "I think so, yes."

"In other words, you'll find out for us who the biggest is; you'll tell us his name."

"I think I can help."

Judge 2020 had to muster all his judiciousness and his judiciary skills to reach his next conclusion. And to his credit, he computed it quickly.

"All right, little SIX. Your questions will be answered, to the best of our ability. But *privately*. You are to remain in *solitary confinement*." And then, after a pause, he elaborated. "In solitary confinement until you help us, or *forever*."

What had he promised them? SIX asked himself. And why?

He was no longer free. He looked around the courtroom, at the marble colonnades, at the wall tapestries, and at the leafy trees that peered in through the tall windows.

Only then did he realize that he had counted utterly on Elizabeth, on seeing her again. But would he? He needed her desperately. On the way out, he took a last look at the audience; they resembled a trellised garden of petticoats. If only he could see her once more. Perhaps she would answer his questions. In his last glance, he saw handkerchiefs of many colors; at least some in the audience were weeping—weeping for him.

13

The Sentence Begins

O N HIS LAST DAY before prison, SIX pinpointed the questions he had to answer. Why were people so often found in the presence of numbers? Was there nothing in the universe numbered without people being involved? Perhaps the answer held the key to mortality, and might even shed light on who the biggest was.

He was going through his library, deciding which books to take, when the doorbell rang. At the door were three unkempt figures in khaki fatigues. Inside his apartment, SIX saw that they had the gift of sprawling and idling in a way that made them seem like a huge crowd. "I'm 32," said the most slovenly of them. "You go to jail tomorrow, and we *admire* that."

"We represent the Sixists," said another. "We're dedicated to helping you escape."

Then SIX observed that some wore patches on their clothes with strange sayings. "EVEN IS ODD." "MONGRELS OF MORTALITY." They were apparently from that intrepid band of radicals, who had been meeting secretly all along.

"I appreciate it, but—"

"You are our figurative leader. You won the vote. We'll soon be known as the Sixists across the whole Republic."

"We're enemies of the Professor," said another. "Have you any money to help us?"

"Help you what?" asked SIX.

They looked puzzled. "Alert the nation to your importance."

"Free you," said the first.

"But it can't be by violence," said SIX, forking over a few small bills that he would no longer need.

"No. We're going to use the Professor's own methods. We're going to beat him by words. To raise money and free you."

As they stood up to leave, SIX recognized 32 as the famous political cartoonist. His sketch of Goodness with a white kerchief, carrying a mop and pail and throwing up at the sight of the Professor, was well known.

When they were gone SIX wondered, how can they possibly raise money? And what did they mean "beat the Professor by words"? Then he forgot all about them.

The Professor held a press conference to announce his plan. He would put both Five and SIX in prison. There they could sample the road ahead. Or the "non-road," as the Professor put it. In reality, time cost nothing, but to someone playing mortality, it could seem very expensive. He would punish SIX at his own game. His staff would answer SIX's questions, but SIX would remain in prison. The irony of the plan appealed to the Professor.

At daybreak the next morning the prison van rolled onward, past mountain laurels and bayberry hedge, and soon the green vegetation was no more.

Five sighted it first—its massive gray walls. Then battlements and towers seemed etched in the sky, and the whole of it grew grayer and grayer as they drew closer. The windows had iron gratings; the promenades and walls rose from a deep foundation. To SIX, the huge gray structure looked like the stump of an elephant's foot left behind in a creek.

Warden Two greeted them warmly. For years a mere figurehead of the Evens Party, he had become a favorite of the Professor's. Though he knew SIX well, he spoke with ruthless impersonality. He assured SIX, "I have seen prisoners packed into cells and underground dungeons, and I can tell you, your upstairs small room is better. This is as good as any private prison."

As they entered the gates, he told SIX, "A staff of experts will answer your questions. The Professor chooses them." He smiled. "You won't see me very often. I'm taking my Masters degree in Penology." It was part of the Professor's incredible program of extension courses for everyone who wanted to advance.

Once inside, Two waved good-bye.

A jailor led Five off. Another, 64, pointed down a long corridor, and when SIX started, he followed. In the darkness, the jailor stumbled. He muttered illiterately, "And this is supposed to be a model penitenterary."

There was a light at the cell door, and SIX could see him. He had a chain with keys of many different sizes. He wore gray work clothes, and was bumpy and pitted. His expression was a perpetual snarl, making him look like a wounded hyena. He was hideously ugly, but SIX did not know this.

There was nothing in the cell but an oil lamp and a stone fountain, and SIX deposited his books and pencils.

A little later, a terrible moan pierced the corridors, and SIX was glad to be out of doorshot.

SIX thought he had to choose his questions carefully; the experts would be coming to answer them. He wondered what it was like to have only a hundred years left. Fifty? Ten? He could not possibly go to her now, hemmed in by a terrible wall. Strangely, he felt he had abandoned her. How could he have done this, at a time when her own happiness was unsure? The knowledge that she was mortal deepened his pain. He wanted to be near her at the moment she discovered she was going to die. It seemed only fair. And to spend time with her afterward, to give her the fact of his SIXness to console her.

He sat down and wrote out his first question, and sent it off to the Professor for his staff to answer. "What is a genius?"

The next day a philosopher arrived at his cell and told him. "Human creatures who discover things. Then they die and others get what they found."

14

Two Incredible Crossword Puzzles

I N THE DAYS that followed, SIX plied the Professor's Committee with a miscellany of questions in different fields. The Professor was forced to summon a wide assortment of experts. Being called meant instant fame, the reward for long years of learning facts that had no relevance except on final exams.

Each day a different staff could be seen trooping after the gnarled 64 toward SIX's cell. Through the dank darkness the clattering of Numberland's leading chemists, botanists, accountants, sociologists, and linguists could be heard over the stone floor. In the light from an occasional gas lamp covered by a tin shade, the experts could see the contours of manacles and grappling hooks hanging neatly on the wall.

Once when they arrived at the dismal but illuminated cell where SIX spent his time, they discovered that one of them was missing. It was an entomologist who had been enraptured by the Castle. The jailors found him in a musty room applauding while a colony of gnats danced in a ray of light. He explained to them patiently that he was not applauding but keeping time for them.

Meanwhile, rumors were rife about why the biggest had not come forward and declared himself. Many experts had concluded: resentment. Whatever his name, he could have no one to turn to—no giants to remove *his* garbage or transfer his home to the country when summer began. Why should he declare himself? Very possibly he was enjoying the irony of their agony.

Then, while SIX was languishing in the Castle, and the public was still reaching for hope, there came the first of two incredible phone calls.

The Professor had just concluded a meeting with his staff when the mysterious caller told him, "I can name our biggest for you."

"Can you really?" The Professor was elated. He informed the others. Hats were thrown in the air.

The Professor said over the phone, "Go ahead."

"Will you give me a million dollars cash?"

"Who are you?"

"What's the difference who I am! I have no desire to meet you or know you," said the voice.

"A million dollars!" The Professor was startled, and repeated the words aloud so that others could know what was going on. Then, realizing that the money would be trivial to so vast a republic, he replied hurriedly, "All right, you've got it. Who is he?"

The voice then uttered something unforgettable. "His name will be the top word in the Sunday crossword puzzle. Next week. We composed it. Send the money to the headquarters of the Sixists."

"The Sixists!" repeated the startled Professor.

"It will be the top word going across," the voice went on.

"Tell us *now*," said the Professor.

"First the money," said the voice. "We wrote it and we'll send in the puzzle as soon as you pay us."

"Please tell us now," said the Professor. "We need to know as soon as we can."

"It will be there Sunday. You'll figure it out from the downs. They're easy. Is it a deal?" The voice sounded reassuring.

Still the Professor hesitated.

The voice went on. "Well, the answers will come out the following Sunday, even if you don't get it right. Okay?"

"That would be a week lost," cried the Professor.

"You'll get it. You'll get it." The voice seemed even more reassuring this time.

"You're sure?"

For a time there was silence. Then the caller repeated a final time, "Is it a deal?"

"Okay," the Professor said reluctantly.

Of course the newspapers ballyhooed the crossword puzzle all week, and there were speculations as to the name of the biggest. By dusk on Saturday citizens surrounded their local newsstands. All had the same idea. They would attack the downs and call in the name. Some saw it as a cheap shot at a great discovery. By sunset on Saturday in every city there were many citizens who rushed to the local offices of the *Daily Printout*. In Numeropolis, at the main office, these gross figures forced their way past the reception desks. One actually got caught in the presses. A shredded number was a rarity, but possible: Immortality ensured at least some coming together of the parts. these pushy figures managed to get on line at the newspaper ahead of all but those hunting for apartments.

Sure enough, under the column ACROSS, number one read: "Biggest creature in existence." It was eleven letters.

A myriad citizens must have rushed almost simultaneously to "One down," and read at virtually the same time "Unsounded letter in mythical dwarf." In the Professor's office, where his staff worked on the puzzle together, the lexicographer knew the answer at once. It was the *G* in the word *gnome* which was unspoken. Clever, that reference to a dwarf in order to indicate the first letter of the biggest giant in the land. So his name began with a *G*.

Even as they labored singly and in groups, the citizens across the land were aware that this was by far the most important crossword puzzle that their nation had ever attempted.

There was no "Two down." However, "Three down," consisting of only two letters, read "Initials of American President."

"What could that be?" asked the Professor indignantly. "First name and last. Tells us nothing."

"Not so." The voice belonged to 24, the cryptographer whom the Professor had chosen to help them. He went to the blackboard and wrote in chalk while the rest watched. Quickly he put down on the board all the possible combinations of American presidents, starting with G.W. and right through A.L., L.J. and R.R., right up to and including the present one.

"Those are the combinations," he said. "It's a greatly reduced list as against all possible pairs of letters.

"We get a break in John Adams and John Quincy Adams having the same first and last initial," remarked the entomologist. "We should be thankful for that."

No one was impressed.

Then the Professor said decisively, "We can rule them both out," and they all turned toward him.

"We can rule them both out, because it says 'initials of American president,' not American president*s*," He accented that last *s*.

That seemed air-tight. Then someone pointed out that the word below was "head covering," in three letters. That gave them *HAT.* and meant that the president began with an *H*.

The Professor sounded upset. "Hays, Harding, Harrison! Damn it!" he shouted. "What a bad break."

"Or it could be *CAP,* said someone.

Concentrating hard was citizen 77, who had been doing puzzles ceaselessly for many years, not just in newspapers but whole books of them. This member of the special Committee could by that time read a book down as easily as across. Even when reading an ordinary book, he always had a sense of what was directly below the words he was reading, and of what was impinging from above, which might give the letters away. It didn't matter that the letters in a book were actually there. Secretly, 77 was hoping for one of those weird-looking three-letter words known only to inveterate puzzle-solvers.

But, unfortunately, there weren't any such words.

More effort, and the team finally arrived at the solution. All those in the Professor's group appreciated the name of the biggest at the same time. The word for "One across" was *GRANDISSIMO.*

"What the hell does that tell us?" asked someone.

"It does mean 'biggest,'" the Professor explained with grudging admiration.

They knew they'd been swindled. But any judge would rule that they had to pay the money.

"All right. So we know his name. But we're no closer to finding him," complained the General.

"Don't be so sure," said the Professor, who seemed to enjoy correcting the General on those rare occasions when the General did speak in the Committee meetings. "The name does have value," said the Professor emphatically. He went on to explain that it helped them conceptualize who they were looking for but couldn't find.

Actually, the Professor was correct about Grandissimo focusing them on the issue. Days later, the public got an even sharper focus when a sportswriter referred to him as "the big G," and the name caught on. The public had pinpointed this all-important figure, and the Sixists had funded their revolutionary movement.

Soon afterward, the Sixists struck again. Realizing that under the Professor the nation had developed an appetite for crossword puzzles, and having exploited that appetite once, they knew that a second phone call would find an even more susceptible audience.

This time the voice said, "Another vitally important entry will appear in Sunday's crossword puzzle if you're interested."

The call was taken by a herpetologist, who had just given the Committee an excellent answer to one of SIX's questions. He happened to be standing near the phone.

"See how much they want this time," said the Professor, who then gave the herpetologist no chance and snatched the phone himself.

"Nothing," the caller told him a moment later. "It will be "Five across" this time. You'll have a week to get it."

"Who's calling?" asked the Professor.

"A Sixist. I'm too big to see you. I live far away. They chose me for my diction."

"Trace that call," said the Professor.

"I wouldn't bother tracing it," said the voice, surmising what the Professor had in mind. "I'm so far away that even electricity would take a long time to reach me."

It was true. Indeed the very big numbers could outrace electricity itself if they wanted to.

That Sunday, attached to the crossword puzzle once again were the words *The Sixists*. However, the entry "Five across" was confusing. It read: "What we'll blow up. To shorten."

"You mean the same word means both of those things?" exclaimed the General. "Impossible."

"Don't you see," announced the cryptographer, "the Sixists are telling us they're going to blow something up. We've got to hurry."

"Well, they ought to tell us or not tell us," remarked the General.

"No," shouted the Professor. "They're playing our game. Trying to use intellect to defeat us. No. We'll figure it out in time to anticipate them. We'll stop them from blowing up whatever they have in mind."

Once again the nation's best set to work, nonstop. A force under the local police chiefs of every city stood ready to act, as soon as the location could be figured out. Nearly everyone was sure the site would be in Numeropolis, since destruction there would be most significant and get the most publicity. The whole nation would learn about it at once. But what were they planning to destroy?

This time the experts labored to no avail.

The following Sunday, a figure could be seen climbing the twisted wire of the bridge to the lower deck. In a fedora hat and with coat collar up, this Sixist paused to look down. Then he deposited a little blue box and left it there.

In the explosion, the smaller figures on the deck were hurtled high into the air like shuttlecocks.

An hour later a citizen called the newspaper elatedly. "I got it!" he cried. "What we'll blow up. To shorten." He paused, to give them their last chance. Then he told them: "ABRIDGE."

If the Professor had feet, he would have kicked himself. They had beaten him at his own game.

As a result of the nation's helplessness, whole cities were now in tears. Word came that figures far away were marching angrily in twos and threes. Several times a shadow hovered over Numeropolis, that of a furious citizen debating whether to trample them. Other citizens stole moments for themselves. It seemed not to matter what they did in the darkness. Sorrow was everywhere.

In response, the Professor arrived at a decisive course of action that might save the nation. It was drastic, but he could see no alternative.

15

Numberland Takes
a Drastic Measure

ANY WONDERED WHERE the psychiatrist 200,001 was. His absence meant two giants not coming forward— Grandissimo, who could easily have removed the interloper overshadowing the Capital, and the psychiatrist, a giant in his field. Reports had the psychiatrist working on his latest theory. Not that his absence led anyone to attack him. Psychiatry was flourishing. As one idea utterly replaced another in the field, the status of those in it kept improving. No system of psychology is ever disproven. They never die; they just peter out. New theories replace old ones as the status of the field rises. And so it was. Everyone respected the profession, but no one missed the doctor; there is nothing so stale as last year's expert.

In the chaos, a new group sprang up known as numerosocial workers. They argued that anyone with anything should give it to someone with nothing: "The least deserve the most." They maintained that in a just republic those now on top would be on the bottom and those with nothing to show would be in their place. As if whatever went wrong had precisely reversed everyone's position. Many wore blue double-knit polyester suits as insignia of their loyalty to the underdog. Chaos was coming to the most orderly civilization in history, and the Professor knew that his moment for drastic action had arrived.

He pushed past photographers and reporters on his way toward the mahogany doors. Knowing his every word was news, all he would say was "No comment today." Inside, 79 was addressing the Committee. "We have two questions from SIX in the Castle—"

"Let's run through them quickly," the Professor broke in. "I have an important announcement to make."

"Is the termitologist here?" asked 79.

8040 stood up.

79 read from his paper. "Does the warrior termite know that the walls he is defending are going to harden, leaving him outside the citadel to die among the enemy?"

"No," said 8040 confidently. "Or he'd be committing insecticide." He sat down and was being congratulated by the others when the Professor hurried them along.

"Last question," he snapped.

It was addressed to 96, the quadruped specialist.

"Do hippopotami die?"

"Well, I've been thinking about it," said 44 slowly, trying to make the most of his moment.

But the Professor interrupted him, speaking very fast. "The answer is yes, but hippos aren't really important. They have only two choices, dry or wet, go in or come out. They don't matter much."

Then he paused and looked over the assemblage. "And

now the announcement. After this SIX won't matter either. We're going to get *rid* of him. Entirely."

They all looked startled.

"We're going to send him so far away," continued the Professor, "that we will lose track of him. Isolation. Absolute isolation. The only question is *where*."

They nearly all accepted the plan at once.

"The bottom of the sea," said 79.

"No. That's not far enough away," said another. "That's okay to punish humans, but not a numerical figure."

"*Ice* on top would slow his return," commented 44.

The General was aghast. "Are you saying 'Send him so far away that we lose touch'?" he asked in astonishment.

"Exactly that," said the Professor, his glasses glinting nefariously. "Each of us will do the additional job of one smaller—"

"That's not the point," interrupted the General. "You know our rules. 'Any figure may be needed at any time. *None* can be removed.'"

"But whose rule is that?" demanded the Professor.

"We've always had that rule. We can't . . ." sputtered the General. He looked around the room. Many felt he was right, as if an unseen presence had laid down the rule. It would be a terrible violation. But no one wanted to go up against the Professor.

"Ice, eh! Not a bad idea," said the Professor.

"What about the North, in the Squillion Territory?" exclaimed 101, holding up a map.

They gathered around him as he went on. "In this land of giants, even quadrillions need to travel with much bigger figures who carry huge flag poles with them." He pointed to a spot off the map. "About here."

They looked aghast.

"Where?" asked the Professor, showing genuine interest.

"But you *can't*," said the General.

"Here," went on 101. "This is a frozen, unexplored region. We have no real map of it, beyond a detail used by the Squillions themselves. No marking under a billion units."

"Good. That will do it," said the Professor. "Agreed?"

They all assented to the spiteful plan, except for the General.

This goes into effect at once," the Professor said. "I think with SIX gone, these radicals will slow down. Order will return."

"How can we have order without SIX?" asked the General.

"We are going to lop off the gangrenous part for the sake of the Republic," said the Professor as they closed their portfolios.

Later, down on the street, the General collected his thoughts. "Education," he muttered to himself. "Education at any cost. That's the greatest delusion we ever had. Education has certainly failed for us." At that moment, he resolved to take matters into his own hands, so to speak.

Evening was approaching. Outside, the descending sun seemed a fearful red, and made the yellow buses look orange. Distraught, the General boarded the wrong bus. On observing that the seats were all too high, he nervously asked to be let off. A few passengers laughed. Standing there, he muttered something about the red sky misleading him.

The bus driver kidded him. "Lost it in the sun, eh, General?"

More passengers laughed. But all the General could think

about was the danger the Professor imposed. Things were bad enough without an act of panic.

That night, the General assembled his best soldiers. They had deposited their guns in the rifle rack and were concentrating hard. He warned them. "Guard against any word you don't understand, or concept said to be too hard for you," he advised them.

"We will," they replied in unison.

"Make them explain everything," warned the General. "Contact our troops in every known city. This is an emergency. We cannot allow a President to remove one of us, even the smallest, from Civilization."

They knew it was urgent, and that the rupture between the President and their leader could not be mended.

Their shufflestep had a little extra zing that day, as they went down the stairs. And they would need it.

16

The Professor Sets the Wheels in Motion

As Two strode between the glass and steel towers of Numeropolis, onlookers recognized him as the figurehead of the Evens Party. Over the ages, the nation had often watched him putting garlands on one of the Twin Fountains in the Plaza every Immortality Day. Prompted by the keen joy of knowing that the Professor had big things in mind for him, he hurried along. Onlookers paused to stare at this tiny figure as he hastened over the pavement, though not much over it. Not only did all know him by sight, his very smallness drew attention to him.

In Numberland, small was beautiful. Their criteria of beauty, as with humans, stemmed from what was socially advantageous, and small figures possessed the everlasting servitude of the large. Had the numbers the power to change size, which of course they did not, most would doubtless have chosen to become smaller rather than bigger. Sociologists would have been studying the phenomenon of "downward mobility"; as it was, however, alterations of size occurred only in dreams, or sometimes on the stage.

In the Professor's lobby, Two saluted the secret service figures and was announced. He then rode up in the elevator, and entered the Professor's multi-level apartment. Finally he was admitted to the highest level, and strode over carpeting as thick as he was. Quite a few apartments in Numberland were more than duplexes; they ran many stories high and had railings so that tall numbers standing on lower floors would not have to stoop while entertaining smaller visitors. This arrangement was like that in certain of our zoos, where people ascend to be at eye level with the giraffes.

The Professor snapped on his ready-made tie, and came into the room. "Well?"

"I've given them your order. The Castle will be emptied by midnight. Only SIX will be left inside."

"Good," said the Professor. "Tomorrow the Castle, with SIX in it, will be sent far away."

He dismissed little Two with a gesture, and the latter departed.

Alone once more, the Professor unsnapped his tie. He thought about those he was about to free from the Castle: first about Five, the artist, whom he'd put there with canvases and paints of every color and then tormented by keeping his cell pitch-black. Whatever splendid murals the artist had in mind would remain sleeping in those tins of paint. In releasing Five, he warned the artist to do meaningful works for the cause of immortality, and for the Republic, or he would lose his light again.

Then, too, in the Castle prison was 45454, the historian who had in the last year become a celebrated lecturer. At the end of every speech 45454 had predicted some horrendous tragedy. Audiences in auditoriums would grow restless, wondering what it would be, until he finally came to it. Each night he foresaw some novel disaster. He'd packed them in, and his more hopeful rivals as lecturers didn't have a chance. His public relations agent had cleverly billed him as "the Pessimist." "Well," the Professor mused, "his most recent lectures had been given in the privacy of his cell, and he, too, had promised to stop his disruptive activities."

Also in the Castle was 69, the pervert whom the Professor had always despised. The Professor didn't like to think about him. His very name was repugnant.

As the Professor reviewed the names of the prisoners, still another figure to be released was 3017, the astronomer, who a few months earlier had been the subject of a controversy that shook the Republic. The Professor smiled when he recalled his choice of punishment for 3017. He had left the figure alone in a turret with his telescope, but without windows in his cell. This was especially appalling for 3017, who was socially a dud, and who would have been a square in any circle except that of his telescopic lens. It was 3017's faultless honesty that had made him such a problem.

The controversy surrounding 3017 proved enormously important. It had begun during a routine astronomical sighting. On the side of a mountain, in a clearing among shadowy pines, 3017 had waited motionless for days, as he often did, draped only in his long astronomer's coat. That night, spry yellow leaves were blowing everywhere. In the moonlight he could see sharply through his optical telescope. He also had at his side his spectrometer, a photometer, and a micrometer. His thoughts, however, kept focusing on his radiometer, which he had mistakenly left home.

Adjusting his instruments, 3017 saw first one and then

many cities of new numbers on a faraway stretch of land that had been barren the night before. They were briefly visible in the moonlight, and then vanished when the moon disappeared behind a cloud. He was sure that he had not been confusing size and distance: They were newly appeared figures. Looking again, he became certain that not just one but a dozen cities he saw were *utterly new*—neither he nor anyone else had ever seen them before. No doubt about it. Brand-new and bigger numbers than those ever seen before were making their appearance.

Though alone on the hillside, he had shouted, "There are *more and more* of us." Then, oblivious to what it might mean to the Republic, he rushed to tell this to the Professor. Running down the hill in a frenzy, almost as if he were afraid he would forget this remarkable discovery, he kept saying to himself, "There are more and more of us. There can be no permanent Grandissimo."

In his excitement to report the discovery, he almost slid down the ragged mountainside.

"Impossible," said the Professor, when 3017 told him.

"But where are they coming from?" asked one of the Professor's aides.

"They couldn't possibly be *new*!" said the Professor.

"Could they?" asked someone else on the staff.

"Yes," claimed 3017. "Yes, yes, yes," he insisted, no matter how many times he was questioned. "If they were there before, at least their *shadows* would have appeared." Adamantly defending his procedures, he kept repeating, "I count the numbers *and* the shadows. They absolutely *weren't there* before."

83

The Professor had replied disbelievingly, "Do some research on it."

And the next thing the astronomer knew, he had been plunged into the Castle with his telescope.

Now he, too, was about to be set free, but only after promising not to say anything to anyone regarding his discovery.

The others to be liberated were lesser figures, whose crimes had been against the language. As a lesson, the Professor had given them short sentences. "We'll never improve our economy until our speech habits become more economical," he thought to himself. "Well, we can absorb all these figures, so long as we dispose of SIX, and that will be tomorrow."

17

SIX Learns the Truth

S TILL, NOT A SINGLE figure had recovered from the fear of mortality. The thought of so many numbers suffering on his account was hard for SIX to bear. He went over his notes painstakingly, and the answers he had received. But nothing. Still nothing. Not a solid clue regarding the status of his race, except for that funny, invariable relationship between numbers and people. Though the tension increased, he knew he had to keep going.

Inside the Castle, the jailor, 64, told SIX about the barracks and the boarded-up places, and the cloistered passage full of dry mold where the entomologist had been found. It seemed to SIX that the jailor himself was becoming more and more upset.

One morning the rain was falling. The jailor was pulling off a soggy boot when SIX asked him, "When will you let me out?"

The jailor took the question hard. "I'm not really a jailor," he insisted. Then he moaned, as if voicing his thoughts to no one in particular. "I didn't realize it would be like this. Keeping you here. Never had any prisoners before." He seemed very upset. "A living *negative*! Me? Saying 'you can not'? Damn." He grew even more distraught. "Damn! Damn! Damn! I hate it. But I *have* to be a negative or I'd be nothing at all."

Over the following days he softened more. SIX himself, since pondering about mortality, had come to feel farther away from some, but in a curious way closer to those who traveled alone. There was real beauty in the jailor's ugliness, a relief from strain, as if he were telling everyone, "None of us likes this imprisonment by beauty, which we all suffer from."

The jailor confided to SIX that he loved music. He brought SIX to his secret room. There, SIX saw an aged piano, its ivory keys were yellow and brown at the edges; they looked like human teeth that needed to be cleaned.

The jailor sat down and began to play folk songs of many regions, one after the other. The "sustain" pedal issued a loud squeak, but neither noticed.

When he'd finished SIX said, "That's wonderful!"

In exultation, the jailor boasted, "And no archipelligos or cheap shots."

Then came the note announcing that the Castle, except for SIX, would be emptied out. By nightfall the rest would be gone.

"What will they do with them?" SIX asked.

"I don't know. It's not good."

SIX said, "But the authorities have to keep answering my questions. That was their promise."

"Yes," the jailor said reluctantly.

"Then, even if they send me somewhere, the Committee

will have to keep sending me my answers," said SIX hopefully.

The jailor looked sad.

"When do you leave?" asked SIX.

"I've decided to stay," said the jailor. "I've got a lot to learn. I hate to leave my piano behind." Those weren't his actual reasons, but then he gave the real one. "I've never met anyone like you. You *listen* to me."

The next morning 22,000,000,000 approached with giant strides. The huge jeweler fumbled through his pockets and removed a map, on a piece of paper far bigger than Numeropolis. As he squinted at it, he remarked to himself. "The Professor says they're supposed to be . . . just about here."

He peered down into the snow. "Better look out for Millionville, and not step on the outskirts; they're hard to see. The land of the tinies can't be far away."

A few steps farther along, he put on a thick eyepiece, then bent low and examined the landscape for details. "The Professor says the 'virus' is over here that's causing all this doubt."

Again he looked at the map, then drew out a pair of minute tweezers. "There it is!" he said to himself, and plucked up the Castle. With it safely in his charge, he hurried off, soon boarding a Tray carried by a much bigger figure.

To SIX and the jailor it sounded like an earthquake. Boulders were breaking below them. A mighty *snap* and they felt themselves rising. Over the parapet of the Castle they saw fleecy clouds.

"We're being kidnapped," cried the jailor.

On and on they went, lifted by carriers of ever increasing

size, higher and higher. And the night found them still ascending through the starry nowhere.

During the flight, SIX listened to the jailor talk about himself. "I would have been a teacher, but I'm allergic to chalk." He told SIX about a dream he had had, which he couldn't get out of his mind. "There was this *duck* with a huge bill coming after me, honking and sure of himself."

SIX told him about the mortality game, and the unsolved mystery relating people to numbers, and about his visits to Elizabeth.

Later, the jailor said, "My goodness, we're higher than the sun. No wonder it's dark."

On and on they went, not realizing it when the descent began.

Hours later, a hard white light flooded the Castle, bringing every cobweb into view, as they never appeared before. Inside, it was as bright as Judgment Day. Both knew at once that they had landed.

"What now?" SIX asked.

Suddenly, they could see the snow rising outside. "Let's get out of here," said the jailor, and they clambered down the cold stone steps as fast as they could, and out onto the snow.

Looking back, they saw that The Castle was sinking fast. The promenades and turrets were already gone. Now they saw the main tower descending, like the periscope of a submarine. Then, of the whole Castle, nothing remained.

The two of them stood alone on the vast surface. Luckily, they were weightless or they, too, would have punctured the crust of snow and gone under. In the blinding glare, they did not even see the huge carrier stalking away, satisfied that he had carried out his orders, having left them in a place that even he could not find again.

The wind howled violently.

"I didn't think it would be like this," said SIX.

"What did you expect? An educational experience?" The jailor was busy cutting off his overalls with a knife. As the clothing went rolling away in the wind, it looked like a figure cut in half.

"Which way?" shouted SIX.

The jailor laughed, as if it were a naive question. "Any direction's as good as any other," he shouted above the din. "Let's get started."

He submitted to his fate with stoic resignation. He had seemed more ruffled the other day admitting his identity as jailor than now, finding himself misplaced in a wilderness of white. "Let's get started," he repeated.

"But suppose we make a mistake?" SIX asked.

"Ha ha ha." The jailor could hardly control his laughter.

"What's so funny?"

"How can we make a mistake if we have no information?" He broke up laughing again. Then he said, "If it's not the right direction, we'll just come back and go twice as far the other way."

"All right. That way." Six pointed off in the distance.

At once they began trudging in silence. Over the glistening surface they went. Sometimes it was so cold that the snow stuck to them. To SIX, more than once, the jailor looked like a snow figure.

They came to a great cliff, so steep that only a number

could climb it, and that with real difficulty. SIX started to change direction to go around it.

"No. That won't do," the jailor warned. "We've got to hold to our course or we won't learn anything."

As they went on, it troubled SIX to think that they might have to retrace all those steps, and their next direction, too, retrace their approach countless times to reach civilization. For a moment he sought refuge in the idea that they were immortal; it meant that sooner or later they would have to reach a city. But what if we were mortal, he thought. We might never return in time. Bravely, he vowed he would not take solace, even then, in immortality, but would live this most isolated and horrendous adventure, even this one, as if he were mortal.

Below, they heard the horrendous noise of chunks of ice tumbling into the channel. Still they kept on. SIX was glad the jailor was there; he dreaded the thought that he might have been alone on this terrible journey. Looking over at 64, he saw that the jailor seemed content. He decided to engage the jailor in talk, and as they forged on through the eddying snow, he asked him more about his life.

The jailor told him, "I've had a lot of good breaks in life, actually. I can't complain, being able to play the piano."

On they went, the jailor looking at times like a pillar of snow.

"How much longer?" SIX asked of himself, but aloud.

"I don't know," said the jailor. "I really have no idea. If I did, I'd tell you."

SIX felt foolish, turning for comfort to one in the same position as he. He was about to apologize when the crackling of

9 0

the ice became deafening, and brought all conversation to a halt.

A moment later he was suddenly lifted, as if at his own command. The sounds of the ice were gone, and he saw the great white surface receding below him.

There was something different about his flight this time, as the whiteness gave way to blue. He was crossing a huge ocean he had never seen. Then he saw soft green hills in the distance, and realized it was the same mortal earth he had visited twice before.

He knew he was headed toward those hills. The countryside was in bloom, and he arrived at a house with high, fancy porches; it had gates and a gable.

Inside at a desk sat a woman. Her hair was combed straight back, her nose seemed to jut out more than before. There were crevices in her cheeks. She looked like a humorous version of her former self. Time had blasted her face.

"Elizabeth!" he said.

"I am glad to see you," she replied. Her voice was deeper than before. "I have given you a lot of thought," she said. "We all have."

"You are famous!" said SIX. "You won the Nobel Prize. I am so proud of you." He wondered how he knew all of a sudden. But he did know this.

"Thank you."

"Tell me how—I mean how you—I mean how people got to recognize you."

She told him she had gone to Princeton and from there to Stanford, where she had finally managed to represent the prime number, which enabled mathematicians to solve many of the problems of antiquity.

"That's why you got the prize, isn't it?"

"Yes." She was surprised he knew. But he understood nothing about mathematics or what she went on to talk about. "I did my original work in palindromic functions," she said. "Like the last digits of the squares of the digits. They make a palindrome. That led to their discovery."

Not a word did he understand. Still he beamed as she spoke. When she finished he said to her, "I'm so happy." Then his whole tone became intensely serious. He said to her "Elizabeth, we've got a tremendous problem. We need you. Can you help us?"

She seemed surprised. But to a genius a problem is a gift, and she said, "I'll try. Give me all the facts."

He took that as a cue to tell her everything he could about Numberland, and she listened with wonderment. He told her about the game, and the trouble he was in for seeing her, and about the Plague of Doubt, as the numbers themselves worried that they might die. And yet they knew that was impossible. When he came to the search for Grandissimo she laughed. He felt flustered.

"Well, who is the biggest?" SIX asked. "That's the first question."

"There isn't any biggest."

"*Isn't* any?"

"No. There isn't any." She laughed again.

"Well, how do we . . . I mean, how do we have a parade?"

"Oh, you get along fine without a biggest."

It was an answer he hadn't expected, or even dreamed could be made.

"You see, we humans create you as we need you. If there was a biggest, then we could always create a bigger one."

He didn't understand.

"Like a million. Suppose you decided that was the biggest. Well, a million and one is bigger. We can always add one, and that's that.

"No biggest!" He still didn't understand why not.

"We create you as we need you," she repeated.

"Incredible!" he said. "No one back there ever dreamed such a thing. *You* create *us*?"

"Yes."

"But we're immortals."

"Who said so?" She leaned back in her chair.

"No?" SIX was astonished.

"No, SIX." And now she became suddenly gentle, knowing how important her next statement would be to him. "I see you have a wrong idea, you and the other figures." She paused before going on. Then she said,

"SIX, you are going to die."

Could he have heard her correctly?

"What? *Me?* A number, a digit. Are you sure?"

"Certainly. You numbers are just human creations. You are as people think of you. No more."

"What?"

"SIX. You exist only in the minds of people. You can never be greater than we. Indeed, you are the measure of our greatness. When we all die, at some time far in the future, then you will too."

"But there's never been a dead number."

"I know," she said softly, knowing how hard it was for him, knowing from her own experience that accepting death is

93

never easy. "But when people are gone your function is gone," she continued. "When the last of us dies, you will all die at once."

Then suddenly it all became clear. No wonder he had all those feelings. Numbers could feel because, like humans, they were mortal. So it hadn't been just a game. He was alive. Limited in time, like a human being after all. They *all* had limited time.

At almost that very moment, he realized, too, that love was possible, since only mortals can love one another. "Do you love me?" he asked.

"I do, SIX," she responded instantly, "with all my heart." And he knew it was true, now that it was possible. Then the thought came to him of the others dying some day, of giants toppling, lying motionless everywhere. That time was coming, however far away, he thought.

"I've got to tell them," he said to her, and she nodded. She knew exactly what he meant.

"No biggest. We're going to die!" he shouted. "What incredible news! Will I ever see you again?"

"I hope so," she replied.

Mortal, he thought, *mortal!* I am going to die, really die; my time is limited. It hadn't been just a game at all.

Flying back at incredible speed, he realized if they wanted life now, they could have it, life just like human existence. If they wanted a parade, they could have that, too, no need to wait for a biggest anymore. Indeed, they had better not wait. If they wanted a parade they had better begin at once, with whoever they could find. And he had better tell them. But how? Always after Elizabeth he'd returned to his starting place, and this time, he knew, he was horribly lost.

On the way back, the dawn seemed more brilliant than any he had yet experienced. To his surprise, he crossed over Numberland briefly. He recognized those tall buildings he'd seen strutting against the sky, but they were far below him now. No one down there would see him, he was so tiny and going so fast.

Then, in horror, he saw far below him giants wandering as if in a dream. Some were crying, and many appeared confused. Outside the cities he saw messengers carrying Trays, apparently lost, going in ellipses, and some inebriated! Then one much bigger than the rest blocked his path, and it seemed he was going to crash. But in an instant he ascended almost vertically, as precisely as if a trigonometer's mind had set the angle, and went soaring over the huge figure.

Evidently, the citizens were desperately confused over the possibility of death. They imagined that life had no meaning unless they could be sure of their future. "Well, they *can* be sure now," said SIX to himself. "They're going to die. All of them. Every one. Their lives are more precious than any of them imagine. I've got to tell them."

18

Panic

S O ABSORBED IN THOUGHT was SIX that he did not realize precisely when the cities disappeared below him; when he next looked down there was only a span of white. Further on, he could discern textures and shades that had not been there before. The great ice floor was cracking. The sun, struggling through the haze, was making its presence felt.

It was the same mortal earth he had left, but now he knew the truth. And they would know it, too, if only he could return to tell them. The new insights he had gleaned from Elizabeth made the breakup of ice on the vast bay seem like a trivial event. What he had to report this time would be louder than the clamor of all the ice in the universe breaking at once. It would be louder than the terrible roar of the torrents that bore the ice away and gave it new life.

Down below he now saw the jailor plodding ahead, over the network of lanes that had suddenly appeared. Despite the maze of angles and lines, 64 had kept to their chosen course.

From high overhead SIX could see that he had. He admired the jailor more than ever, and was eager to tell him the news.

"I've got the answers. I saw her again!" SIX shouted.

"Really?" said the jailor. "I didn't know you were gone."

He was passing over a ravine still choked with snow, and now SIX was at his side.

"We've got to hurry!" said SIX. "If I tell them, I can save them, save what's left of their lives. Hurry. We've got to get back."

"I don't know what you mean," said the jailor.

"I was there again. She looked different. It was incredible!" He described the changes in Elizabeth and told the jailor everything she had said to him. "She's famous for her work with us. World famous! Oh my friend, we're going to die."

"Really," said the jailor. "That's interesting." Their words echoed through the huge cave that they had just entered. The two figures seemed insignificant amid the stalagmites and stalactites, which made the cave look like a mouth that could have crunched them if it were alive and mortal as they were.

"That explains a lot," said the jailor.

"What?"

"Well, I was looking ahead on the ice. And again I had that vision. In the white surfaces I could see that duck with a huge bill coming after me, honking and certain of himself. Now I know what it is. It's death."

After telling the jailor all the details SIX said jubilantly, "I'm going to see her again. I know I will."

For the first time ever, he saw the jailor look sad.

"We've got to hurry," SIX repeated. "I've got to tell them."

"All right," said the jailor. "That ice floe is going exactly our way. Let's get on it."

Quickly they mounted it, and to their delight, it maintained its course in the swiftly flowing stream.

Back in Numberland, the Professor spoke into a gaggle of microphones at a press conference. "We have excluded SIX from the Republic. Our order remains unchanged, however."

It was a stunning announcement. As the reporters gathered around, some big figures could be seen inadvertently blocking the view of smaller numbers who worked for the lesser newspapers, making it hard for the latter to take photos or ask questions. Still, the flurry of questions touched all relevant issues.

"Who will be sent away next?"

"No one. I promise you that only SIX will ever be disposed of. I want to announce that our Republic will not suffer. You will each do the work of the citizen one unit below you."

"Do you think you'll ever find Grandissimo?"

The Professor answered too quickly. "Yes. And during my semester in office. I guarantee it." The instant he said this he knew he was not on firm ground.

Meanwhile, across town in the Hall of Records, 84, the chief librarian, was dashing through the marble halls. He was the sort who kept on his vest and jacket during the hottest days, and would never cheat by undoing even a single button or loosening his tie. He was so meticulous that he was prone to hysteria if a library card went into its jacket upside down. Imagine his reactions on observing that not one but *two* figures, SIX and 64, had no whereabouts listed.

Through the heavy building he stormed, alerting everyone.

Librarians unseen for ages emerged from behind stacks of books in the archives, painters came down from their ladders, all to stare at the two blank lines in the big book.

After the librarian's call, tiny Two handed a note to the Professor, who momentarily stopped talking with the press to read it. In a state of shock, the Professor told them, "The jailor is gone too."

The uproar almost drowned the reporters' questions.

"Where is 64?"

"With SIX, presumably." The Professor had trouble mustering an artificial smile, but managed to do so.

"And exactly where is SIX?"

"In the Castle?"

"You promised us there'd *never* be another!"

It was obvious he had lied to them.

Then, to his horror, the Professor saw standing in front of him 3017, in his long astronomer's coat. Despite his promise of silence, the astronomer felt actuated by the need to reveal the truth. Even before 3017 ran to the microphone and started shouting, the Professor knew what he was going to say.

"Let me speak. Let me speak. We'll *never* find Grandissimo. There are more and more of us. We're being born. I don't know where we're coming from."

That broke the crowd into a panic.

"When will we ever be immortal and under control again?" someone asked.

"Never!" the multitude seemed to answer in unison.

"Then what's the use?" someone cried.

From buildings everywhere crowds of figures poured forth. Some got into buses, but when traffic stopped they took to the streets, hurrying across the outskirts. Shouts were heard.

"Order is gone." "Immortality is gone." "Our reason for living is gone." "What's the purpose of it all?"

Across the city, the numbers, without any assurance of an eternal next day, were collapsing en masse, and the sight of them panicked the rest, who were running like buffaloes. Many wore heavy leather jackets to withstand the severest conditions. Some had been stomped by the heavy-duty boots of bigger figures, but hurriedly got up and continued the mass exodus from the city. And still they swept on, moaning, doubting their own immortality, seeing no possible existence without it. The panic everyone had feared had come at last.

Out of buildings they rushed, not pausing to help one another, some shouting, "Chaos has come," as if it were totally imposed from the outside. From within a skyscraper could be heard fearful bangings. Though citizens were locked inside, no one stopped to open the doors from the street. Then a pipe burst and flooded a thoroughfare, lifting small figures and sweeping them along, so that they saw only the tops of buildings. Actually, for the tiny figures, the view from the flood was better since so many buildings in Numeropolis were flat at the bottom and gorgeously adorned up near the top, where those figures never saw them. At least, now the diminutive citizens being carried along could enjoy the architecture of those high-blooming buildings.

Their shouts amid the chaos bespoke the fears that had broken loose across all of Numberland. "What is our future?" "How can we go on unless we know?" "We've got to get out of here or we'll all be trampled." Pandemonium was everywhere.

During all this, the General was notably absent. Where he was to be found order still prevailed. He was drilling his troops, including figures of every known size. Their precise time included a silent shuffle in place so as not to break their rhythm while he gave commands. His better-known speeches were punctuated by a crisp stamp in unison at the end of a sentence, and two stamps to accent a very important one. Nor was there ever a sound while he spoke—that would be tantamount to saying, "We've heard it before." The whole nation watching this precise troop on television had been so impressed that they forgave the General his inability to remember the two parts of a question.

There was silence as the General addressed them. "You know who we're looking for. SIX and 64. Probably together. Now they don't call you the Perfect Battalion for nothing. I *know* I can count on you."

Many had ski equipment. Everything was windproof and water repellent. Some wore trappers' boots and goosedown masks; indeed, an onlooker could tell their numbers only from their size. The General, being among the smallest, couldn't gauge them by their altitude alone and had to trust his lieutenants, but did so implicitly. In addition, they carried long identification poles, to plant near their position, which also served as skis, the very equipment they had used to locate 700,000,000,000,000 when he seemed hopelessly lost in the vast wastes of a much bigger land. Obviously, the task confronting them now was harder; indeed, some of the smaller figures in the troop had never seen active duty before.

Their method would be for the big to bear the small, and deposit them with poles at various sites. After scouring a region, the little ones would be picked up and relocated, and they would do this until the missing figures were found.

The General informed his troops that the cities were in

panic. Then he left them at attention while he chatted with some of his chief officers. He could be seen calmly holding up a map that his lieutenant had given him. "We're looking for a sunken Castle in frozen Squillionland," he announced to the little group. He thought to himself, "Good. It's so cold there that I couldn't lose my temper even if I tried." Then he addressed his army once more. "We are ready. Nothing takes forever. Good luck."

With that, his troops began gathering each other up, and soon they were gone, the giant steps of the biggest becoming a muffled roar in the distance.

19

Destruction

THAT NIGHT SIX and the jailor could see nothing beyond an occasional chunk of detached ice moving along with them, though once the jailor pointed to a distant iceberg, its white sides glistening in the moonlight. But the morning brought visions, the splendor of mist rolling around a mountain, and then bare trees that stood against the cold. Then SIX imagined he saw below them a porpoise thumping and squeaking. Could it be? Yes, it was. He somehow felt a kinship with that creature that he never had before, the kinship of being mortal companions.

Then the jailor clutched SIX excitedly and pointed, and they saw two numbers off in the distance of almost unthinkable size. But soon they were gone, and some small russet houses appeared and vanished, too, as if the spool of time were eager to retract them. Everything was richer now even than when he'd played the mortality game; the most trivial sights were daubed in beauty and glorious sadness. "So they keep creating us," SIX thought. "Well, we're here and that's the important thing."

He turned to the jailor and asked, "Are you worried about death?"

"Why worry about it? It's a sure thing," said the jailor. "You don't have to worry."

After hearing a few more questions the jailor told him warmly, "You've got to learn that with limited time, not all your questions will be answered, SIX." And then they grew silent, for a long while watching the shore for signs of numerical life.

However, they saw nothing more. By nightfall the water had risen and their snow float was only half its earlier size. Ahead, the river was about to change course, and they had to disembark. Over the water they headed. Being weightless, they were impervious to the current, but now they had to proceed more slowly. In their path lay a cliff very steep and covered with cedars. During the ascent both wondered how they would know when to turn back and try another direction.

The jailor was the first to reach the top. "Hooray!" he shouted.

Off in the distance they saw a circle of tents and a campfire, and silhouettes of figures moving busily. Near the bivouac was a huge identification pole for much bigger figures to see. It was obviously a search party.

By the time SIX and the jailor arrived, the figures were all inside, but they quickly came out, and danced and shouted at the sight of the missing figures. Then the General himself appeared and was delighted. "I told you they'd be together," he said to a lieutenant. "We're all here!" he exclaimed with gusto.

Some of the explorers told SIX and the jailor about the

chaos in the Republic, about the refusal of the citizens to go on striving for decency until they got more definite knowledge concerning their future. SIX and the jailor listened with wonderment.

Then the General came by and took another look at the two of them, as if to be sure. "We're all here," he repeated. "Now back to the Capital. All is not lost. We'll do what we can to rally the citizens."

"I think I can help you do that," said SIX. "If you'll let me speak to the multitudes, I can persuade them to return."

Stunned, the General looked at the tiny figure who had given the Republic no end of trouble. "You?" he asked in astonishment.

"Yes. I've got some wonderful new information. With what I've learned, I think I can give them reason to come back."

"Let me think about it on the way," said the General. It seemed farfetched, and he had no substitute plan, but still . . .

On the way back, SIX chatted with their giant carrier over the intercom, one who had taken over and was bearing a great many others.

"Well, the easiest way to tell you who I am is this," the giant replied. "I'm 111,111,111,111 times itself exactly that many times."

"What an incredible coincidence!" exclaimed SIX.

"Can't you be a little more polite than to say the obvious? I was hoping a number as little, as revolutionary as you would be above that." He sounded hurt.

"I'm sorry," SIX said. Then he turned to his friend the jailor and remarked, "Wow! Are we far away from home!"

After that when SIX tried to speak to the carrier, the latter wouldn't answer him. Evidently, the giant was in a snit.

After that SIX overheard him telling another passenger he came from a town called Equalville, the capital of a very big province. "About a million of us there," the giant told him. "We're almost all exactly the same size. A few million units among us don't mean nothin'," he explained.

Soon afterward he announced that he was turning the Tray over to a smaller carrier. "Sorry we lost a little time off schedule, but these shoes really hurt." The long descent had begun.

Approaching Numeropolis, they could discern many small fires in the distance. Over the intercom came the voice of their last carrier, in deep pain. "It's terrible. Terrible! They're looting, stealing, *running wild*. It's a stampede. We can't go back there."

Then the General's voice came over the loudspeaker. He was talking to a division of his troops. "You're the biggest in the whole area. You soldiers have your orders. Get ready. We are descending fast."

Now those on board could see frame houses without roofs. Power poles had been knocked over, and electric wires sparked the ground. Buildings were in ruins, a suspension bridge was partly submerged, and through the wreckage ran figures of all sizes.

SIX looked over to see the General at his side. "Words won't do it," said the General. "Look down there. And listen."

Now what had sounded like a dull moan became the pitiful cries of distraught citizens, the agony of thousands who appeared and were gone, running in every direction.

"But I have something special to tell them," pleaded SIX.

The General didn't seem to hear him. He was concentrating

with disgust on the proceedings below. "They're acting as if their number's up," he said indignantly.

Again he addressed his troops on board. "Remember, we have a force of figures ten times as big as they are. When we land we restrain them. Forever, this will be known as the battle for Numeropolis. I have—"

Just then the Tray dipped abruptly. Fortunately, the bubble was intact, or many of the passengers would have slid off into the night. Then they heard their carrier's frantic voice. "It's over. It's all over. We're finished. Cities everywhere are collapsing just like this one. 2,000,000,002 is on the loose. And others even bigger are coming this way." He was sobbing.

"All right. What have *you* got to tell them?" the General asked SIX.

"I'll give them *reason* to come back, to restore order, to *try*."

"What reason?"

"I can't explain it all now. But you can assure them of a parade."

"We trusted the Professor's words, and look what happened," said the General. Then, realizing what SIX had said, he exclaimed, "A parade! How can we have one? You've found Grandissimo? We are truly all alive? Proof that we'll live forever?"

"I said I can give them assurance," said SIX. "The kind of assurance they need to give life a *meaning*. It will be richer and better for them from now on. And yes, they *can* have a parade." For the first time in his life he had been discreet, and wondered whether he had actually lied. Then he was sure he had not.

"All right," said the General. "I don't know what you have in mind. But we have nothing else. We're with you."

*   *   *

When they landed, night had fallen, and the riots were in full force. On the street, SIX and the jailor could see figures running through the rubble, carrying furniture, radios, TV sets. Windows were smashed and merchandise was strewn on the streets. Shadowy figures were filling bottles from a gas pump, then hurling them through car windows, causing blinding explosions. Tiny Two came toward them, carrying a stamp machine from the post office.

"Why are you doing this?" asked SIX.

"I couldn't carry any furniture," replied Two. "It's all too heavy."

"I mean why are you stealing?"

"I'll be truthful with you," Two answered. "Everyone is taking what they can. Why not? There may be no tomorrow. I might as well—" And with that he hurried off into the shadows.

There were sirens, and Numeropolis police cars rolled around a corner. But the officers didn't get out; they were just looking. One of them flashed a light on SIX. "How come you didn't steal anything?" he asked, annoyed.

SIX was baffled. Then down the long avenue came the General leading his National Guard, in their impressive uniforms. The rioters continued throwing bricks and stones, and then one figure ran down the street, dragging some suits much too big for him.

"We've got to stop them," said the General to a lieutenant.

"How?" came the reply. "We can't shoot them, General. They're not people."

"This is happening all across the Republic," said another figure.

108

Then the crowd, scurrying in all directions, was surprised to hear an announcement blaring from many microphones being held by giants. Over the improvised sound network came the General's voice, which was also being sent by radio across the Republic.

"Attention. We have found the missing figures. Go back to your places. There will be a parade. Repeat. There *will be a parade.*"

At first the figures paid no attention, but then came the words, "We have tremendously important news. SIX will address the Republic. Only be patient."

Slowly, the citizens stopped what they were doing. Their questions showed confusion. "Well, what can this mean?"

"It means they've found the biggest."

"Tremendously important news, he said."

The voice boomed again. "Only go back to your places. Your time is coming."

The police and the General's National Guard offered transportation to anyone lost, and provisions were made to house the homeless that night. Reluctantly, first a few and then more citizens returned. But not one put down an item he had stolen. Nearly all were cynical. All right, they would wait—they would hear what SIX could offer them on behalf of the Republic. But it had better be good. After all, how could SIX resolve their future? And without a future, what was the present worth?

The next day giants removed debris and brought in makeshift houses. They were spurred on by the thought that by nightfall they, too, would have a fabricated home instead of the shambles they had created. The stench from the fires and upturned garbage was atrocious, even though giants at the outskirts of cities waved great wads of paper to create a wind and banish it.

Then, even as Numeropolis was being put back in order, word came that spectacularly big figures had gone back to their own cities, too, and would listen to SIX's speech over their radios, since so many of the television stations had been torn down. In spite of the cynicism, many were dismayed by the thought of the riot and its aftermath. They yearned for SIX to offer them real hope in any form. And their curiosity about Grandissimo was so great that they could hardly wait for the next day to come, which many already knew would be the most important day of their lives.

20

SIX Gives His Speech

THE NEXT MORNING, a few hours before the time scheduled for SIX's speech, dry yellow leaves were wafting down from the trees around Central Plaza, at the heart of Numeropolis. Some caretakers raked them; others could be seen busily erecting a podium, and still others were rigging microphones with loudspeakers all around the park. Slowly, the crowd gathered, and were surprised to see on the platform a big clock with people where numbers would be on human clocks. This gold-ornamented clock had gorgeous portraits of Mozart and Shakespeare and Moliere, and Galois the genius mathematician who died at twenty-one. These vivid portraits in color went around the clock in order of how long those marvelous humans had lived, so that Galois's was the first there, and Michelangelo's was the last face that the huge dial hand would reach before it rotated again. Of course, Five had conceived of that clock and created it—everyone knew that at once.

Meanwhile, outside of Numeropolis, giants took portable radios and stood where they could view the spectacle using field glasses; some of the faraway giants used telescopes. Thus the citizens themselves formed a huge stadium, ever widening, as they took size-places for the good of all. More and more appeared, until every single number that any human ever thought of was there, including even the haziest and most borderline figures.

When the General appeared on the platform, cheering burst forth, and even faraway citizens found themselves applauding; then came the Professor, who took his seat in silence. When the astronomer appeared he too was applauded, which only confused him, and he had to be shown to his chair. Then, one by one, a few politicians came, who knew exactly where to sit but little more.

Finally, SIX appeared in his blue suit, and the Professor whispered something to him—the advice to enunciate each word and to pause for emphasis. SIX nodded and advanced toward the microphone, not knowing exactly how to begin.

"My friends," he said, as confidently as he could. However, the noise of the multitude continued. Then he did what the Professor had suggested: Though he wanted to rush forward, he became silent, utterly silent.

Some voices were heard to say, "Hush, I can't hear." "What did he say?" And then, lo and behold, the multitude fell silent, too, waiting for his words.

"My friends, I am here to tell you the most important fact of your life. It is a terrible fact. But it is a wonderful fact too. Oh my friends, you are going to die!"

Pausing, he could hear his echo in the stunned silence, and his own last words frightened him. Then he went on.

"It doesn't matter how big you are. We exist only because humans create us. When the last human mortal dies we, too,

112

must come to an end. Our society will be no more. We are their children."

This time the world *children* echoed throughout the republic. SIX wondered, why weren't they speaking, making any sound at all? Were they really there and listening? He went on,

"And when people die, when they stop thinking of us, imagining us, we die too. Think of it. There is no biggest, no Grandissimo, and there *never* will be. That is because humans don't want a biggest. They go on creating us. There are more and more of us."

The astronomer's very words.

Now, as SIX spoke, he felt inexorably alone, though his truth concerned everyone. He was alone and not. And from that fact itself came a burst of emotion, and now he was shouting.

"But death also means much for us, which we must not lose. It means we can have a parade. We don't have to wait for the biggest anymore. In fact, we had *better* get started, and soon. We can have the society we want. But we had better do it now."

Something perverse about this terrible announcement made the citizens elated. Slowly, the fact of death itself, death for *them*, made them feel giddy, as if for the first time they possessed this truth and it freed them. Even to say that life itself floated in space gave them a kind of certainty, a sense of themselves as heroes, and as smart in giving all to what they had. Many thought about their jobs, and about friends they had neglected, and about the cities themselves, their order, their splendor. Avidly, they waited for more. But SIX had finished. There was nothing more.

The General then announced that the parade would be held the next day, after which they would go back to their posts.

As the reality settled in, the populace felt released from care. It was a bonus that there was no Grandissimo. In their hearts they had never wanted one. And death itself seemed to provide a frame for the magnificent picture of life.

First a few and then more citizens began to applaud SIX for the liberating truth he had brought, and they were thankful that even the weariest river winds somewhere safe to sea. They knew they would rebuild their society on a firmer basis.

While SIX descended from the platform, the picture of Elizabeth's red crib floated before him more clearly than he had remembered it, and those yellowish pages glued on the walls of her room, and her voice during the last visit, still reassuring. It must have been like this for her when she spoke to the auditorium full of scholars. He recalled the thumping sounds he had heard before that second visit to her, which had sounded like horse's hooves; no, he now knew that he had been hearing the noiseless foot of time, and that he could hear it whenever he chose to listen.

Then the sadness was gone, and he thrilled to the rush of power he had experienced while addressing the vastest audience ever assembled. He had an urge to address them once more, for them to gather once more, but of course that would never happen. Some day he would be dead, he knew that. But now he was alive, tingling with vitality, truly in his prime. And he allowed himself to savor the exhilaration of the telling speech he knew he had made.

21

❖

The Parade

❖

THE PARADE ROUTE started just outside Numeropolis and ran past innumerable cities. There had been marches in the past—for instance, every Immortality Day, when a great many residents took part. But never before had there been a show of every single citizen in the Republic. Their starting places were to be indicated, and for many their participation ended when they reached their home cities. The inhabitants of Numeropolis were to be the first to start and the first to stop, being the smallest, with relatively bigger numbers joining in only later on, when the stride of the marchers had lengthened. Knowing now that they were the children of humans, they decided to leave certain technical details to human imagination.

Chief among their decisions was what clothing to wear. The Parade Committee had met at length around the mahogany table and finally reached their decision. That morning the citizens were told over the radio, "There is to be no official outfit for the marchers. After all, this parade is for you." They decided to call it the Mortality Day Parade, and to celebrate Mortality Day yearly, so that the citizens would never forget the great advantages of being alive.

When SIX arrived at the meadow, many were already milling about, and he saw harlequin colors everywhere. He saw buttoned robes, and plaited caps, and green cloth doublets, Spanish capes and brocaded gowns—whatever the individual citizens had always wanted to wear. Apparently, Dr. 200,001, in silk chiffon, was not the only one who elected to don the clothing of human females; the recognition of their mortality freed others citizens to indulge themselves that way as well.

As the gathering figures chatted together amiably, they shared a sense that their near tragedy had unified them. Some thanked SIX for his discovery. In fact, SIX, in his torn green sweater, was the only one who had given no thought to his appearance on that special occasion. Seeing the gorgeous colors all around him, complementing the magic of the day, he realized for the first time that appearances, too, are part of reality, and felt bad that his memory of the parade would not be enhanced by a sense of himself in finery of any kind. He resolved not to make that mistake again, that since time was limited he ought to pay attention to the surfaces of things and not only to their depths.

As throngs of numbers began appearing, the joviality mounted. They could hardly wait to start their celebration. It was as if the nation had just won a war. They began wondering why their individual starting places were not indicated as the General had promised, since they saw no markings on the ground. Then SIX and the others were astonished to see an ever narrowing khilum rug unrolling toward them, propelled by smaller and smaller figures on the Parade Committee. Joyously even some of the digits pitched in, as the rug came to its end. On it they saw their spots indicated clearly in chalk, and began to take their places.

"Not yet!" exclaimed the General. "Not till the band starts." Then the orchestra, spread throughout their ranks, struck up an elated rhythm, and the parade was on.

It wasn't a perfect parade. There were some wiseacres. At one point Nine and Ten interchanged places, just to be out of order for a moment, since life was short; and some giant numbers, it was reported, did the same thing. But all these figures quickly resumed their rightful positions to show that they had not intended even a symbolic rebellion. After all, as they sensed, it is sometimes even more courageous to accept one's lot than to deny it. And after all, their size-places were their lot. Their greatness lay in the fact that they had a place and yet were unique. To know their place was to know themselves.

As they marched along, the music seemed a part of existence; it was so pure they felt it had always been there. Even the Professor swayed to its magic. And so did the General; though he could not be passive and let it wash over him, he consented to it by pretending to conduct it, as if responsible for its beauty. Sheerly from embarrassment, once or twice he broke out laughing.

That day, even the smallest of them felt like humans who conjure up the picture of loved ones deceased and of ancients and prehistoric mortals and those yet to come, picturing them all as alive at the same time, marching in defense of mortality. Thus, though a terrible truth clutched them that day, it did not daunt any of them. They possessed it as firmly as it possessed them.

And on they marched, knowing that all their citizens were taking part and that all would die. Farther along, viewing the parade from high overhead, one could see only the tops of the bigger ones through the great gaps in the clouds.

It did not take the numbers long to rebuild their cities. They reconstructed them with as much order and precision as before, but this time with joy. Their foundation was firmer than it had ever been before. To the Professor's credit, it should be added that at a splendid social gathering he went over to the General and apologized to him in front of everyone present.

"I'm sorry. I've overestimated formal education."

The General was holding a dictionary, something he'd never done before. He looked up from the big book, apparently having found the word he was searching for.

"You have been ophidian, but you're forgiven," said the General.

"'Ophidian,' what the hell is that?" asked the Professor, using profanity for the first time.

"'Pertaining to, or relating to a snake or a serpent,' said the General, reading to him from the book, and they both laughed.

The Sixists continued to meet; they had enjoyed their group so much they would not stop. But they altered their name to "Apathetics Anonymous."

Naturally, the *Daily Printout* covered the parade in great detail, celebrating it. Soon afterward the *Printout* adopted the motto ALL FACTS ARE FRIENDLY.

SIX was given a lifetime chair in philosophy. Not long afterward, he heard a figure talk about the "former Elizabeth Smith." The figure said something about leukemia. The numbers made her birthday a national holiday. She was later put on the clock, which was reproduced in every size and seen ever after across the Republic. At first it pained many figures to see Schubert replaced, but it was pointed out that the clock, like art and life itself, was organic; this had been Five's idea at the start when he constructed it, and its very nature would be a reminder to them all that time was limited, even for them. Their solution would be to delight in the time that remained.